THE BALLAD
OF
LUCY WHIPPLE

THE BALLAD OF LUCY WHIPPLE

BY KAREN CUSHMAN

Clarion Books ✦ New York

Clarion Books
a Houghton Mifflin Company imprint
215 Park Avenue South, New York, NY 10003
Copyright © 1996 by Karen Cushman

The text is set in 13/18-point Horley oldstyle.
Title calligraphy by Iskra.

For information about this and other Houghton Mifflin trade
and reference books and multimedia products,
visit The Bookstore at Houghton Mifflin on the World Wide Web
at (http://www.hmco.com/trade/).

Printed in the USA

Library of Congress Cataloging-in-Publication Data

Cushman, Karen.
The ballad of Lucy Whipple / by Karen Cushman.
p.   cm.
Summary: In 1849, a twelve-year-old girl who calls herself Lucy
is distraught when her mother moves the family from Massachusetts
to a small California mining town, where Lucy helps run a rough
boarding house and looks for comfort in books
while trying to find a way to get "home."
ISBN 0-395-72806-1
[1. Frontier and pioneer life—California—Fiction.
2. Family life—California—Fiction.   3. California—
Gold discoveries—Fiction.]   I. Title.
PZ7.C962Bal   1996
[Fic]—dc20   95-45257
CIP
AC

BP   10   9   8   7   6   5   4   3   2   1

100014

For my parents, Arthur and Loretta Lipski,
who brought me west,
and for Phyllis

ALSO BY KAREN CUSHMAN

Catherine, Called Birdy
The Midwife's Apprentice

THE BALLAD OF

OF

LUCY WHIPPLE

CHAPTER ONE

SUMMER 1849

*In which I come to California, fall down a hill,
and vow to be miserable here*

"Mama," I said, "that gold you claimed is lying in the fields around here must be hidden by all the lizards, dead leaves, and mule droppings, for I can't see a thing worth picking up and taking home." I did not say it out loud, but I sorely wanted to, for I was sad, mad, and feeling bad. The rocking wagon had upset my stomach, my bottom hurt from bouncing on the wooden seat, and my head ached from too much sun and too much emotion.

It was a hot day in late August, and nothing was moving in the heat but the flies, when our wagon pulled out of the woods and stopped at the edge of the ravine.

Dense evergreens towered above us, the hillsides so dark with them the mountains seemed almost black, while over all the fierce yellow sun burned in the blue bowl of the sky. All was silent, with an impression of immensity. Later, folks would call it majestic, noble, imposing, magnificent. But not me.

"Awful," I said, climbing out of the wagon. "Just awful." And I thought with longing of snug spaces, of tree limbs that touched the ground and enclosed safe places within, of the big chair in Gramma Whipple's parlor cozy with the curtains pulled around, of the solidity of Grampop's strong arms and rock walls and houses with porches.

"California Morning Whipple, quit your mooning and come here and help me," Mama called, so I wiped my sunburned face with the back of my hand and went to help.

We woke up the little ones and they, along with the mule and the loaded wagon, were pushed and pulled down the narrow ravine path to the bottom. Sierra, being only two, fell once or twice, so Butte, acting grown-up now he was ten, put her on his shoulders and continued pulling back on the wagon so it didn't move too fast. I fell too, but since there was no one to help me, I brushed the dust off my apron and took to skittering down again with Sweetheart, the mule, beside me.

Finally, in a burst, we skidded down the last feet of the trail to a stop. Everyone, including Sweetheart, was hot and sweaty and dirty. Everyone, *especially* Sweetheart, was tired and hungry and glad to be done.

Mama and I stood and looked at the settlement along the river. The air, heavy with heat and dust, burned my nose and stung my eyes.

"Oh, my, look at this place, California," Mama said.

I looked. The ground was sunburned and barren except for patches of scrub here and there. Small tents, shacks, and brush-covered lean-tos huddled along one bank of the river. On the dirt path that served as the only street, several large, tattered tents shifted in the wind. The biggest had *sulune* painted across its front—*saloon*, I figured, spelled wrong but people seemed to have gotten the meaning all right, judging from the noise inside. The hot wind howled; the tents flapped and creaked; thick dust mixed with the smoke from a hundred cook fires, tinted red by the setting sun. Surely Hell was not far away.

I took Mama's hand. We'd go home now, of course. How disappointed she must be.

Mama and Pa had long dreamed of going west, even to naming their family for western places: me, the first, California Morning Whipple; then Butte, Prairie, Sierra, Golden Promise, the lost baby Ocean, and Rocky Flat, the dog.

When Pa and Golden died of pneumonia the autumn of 1848, people told Mama, "You got to stop dreaming, Arvella, settle down, and take care of them kids." But

Mama was not one to listen to what she didn't want to hear—mule stubborn, her own pa used to call her. After grieving for a spell over what was lost, she took a deep breath and started to look toward what was to come. Butte, Prairie, and Sierra were caught up in her excitement, but for weeks I lived in fear of what Mama would do, for our small Massachusetts town fitted her like a shoe two sizes too small. At night I had dreams of fierce storms that blew us to desert islands, of whirlwinds and whirlpools, of great sea monsters that swallowed the whole Whipple family, including Rocky Flat.

Mama had no patience with what she called my wobblies. She sold the house and stable and feed store, gave the dog to Harold Thatcher at the mill, packed us up like barrels of lard, and in the spring took us on a ship with raggedy sails to seek our fortune in the goldfields of California.

When we arrived near broke in the mud and garbage that was the Bay of San Francisco, Minnie Oates, who had come from Connecticut to fetch her husband, said, "Face facts, Arvella. My hogs lived better than this. You best come back east with us." But Mama wasn't going back. We lived on that idle ship for eight more days, its captain and crew having abandoned it for the goldfields, while Mama stalked through San Francisco in her black dress, new flowered hat on her head and a copy of *The Emigrant's Guide to the Gold Mines (25 cents, 12½ cents without the map)* tucked in her reticule, talking to everyone who would talk back and finally getting herself a job running a boarding house in a mining town. We took a steamer to Sacramento and then to Marysville, where she bundled up us kids in a wagon, bargained a shopkeeper her copper pot from Gramma Whipple for a mule, and trudged three days through country jagged with hills and mountains, peaks and valleys, blazing sunshine and cold sharp nights.

All along the way I watched for the gold lying on the ground, the fruit hanging from the trees, the magical possibilities that Mama said awaited us in California. I saw nothing but evergreens, dirt, and sun—hardly even another human being except for some Indian women grinding acorns by the side of the road. They looked up as we passed, and their tattooed faces frightened me so that I spent the rest of the journey under my old sunflower quilt, crying for my pa and my home and all that was dear to me. And that's how we came to Lucky Diggins, after six months on ship and steamer and wagon, with everything we owned in two horsehair trunks and a straw basket formerly used to carry chickens in.

And here we were. Mama sighed. "Look at this place," she said again. "Ain't it grand?"

"Oh, Mama. Grand?" It looked to me like the wilderness where Jesus was tempted by the Devil. "You said we'd find our fortunes, but I don't see any gold. Only rocks and holes and lizards."

"Look around, California," Mama said. "Look at the

color of the grass, the light trapped in the cracks of the mountains, the sun setting over the peaks. There's gold all around us if you just look."

"Mama, I *am* looking. I'm looking for the school, the library, the *houses*. Mama, I want to go home."

Mama looked up at the big trees and the mountains and the clear blue sky and smiled. "We *are* home, and we are going to be happy here."

I looked down at the dirt. Happy? Towed like a barge around two continents? With no Gram or Grampop? No friends, no school, no big bedroom with Gramma Whipple's quilts on the bed and an apple tree old as Moses outside the window? Happy? Not on your life.

Dear Gram and Grampop,

Well, we are here, me having puked my way down the east coast of the States, around the entire continent of South America, and up the west coast to California. Your daughter Arvella and Butte and the babies had what the sailors called sea legs and were all over that ship. All I saw for five months was the bottom of the bunk above me. I have got very skinny. Butte says I look like a stewed witch.

Mama got herself a job running a boarding house for Mr. Scatter, who owns the saloon and the general store here in Lucky Diggins. He said he was peddling whiskey from a wagon and this is where the mule died so this is where he stayed. The boarding house is a tent. So are the saloon and the general store. I think if you die here and go to Heaven, it too is a tent. Only bigger.

Lucky Diggins isn't much of a town—just tents and rocks and wind. Besides Mr. Scatter, his grown daughter, Belle, and ourselves, the only inhabitants seem to be prospectors with loud voices and dirty faces, porcupines and grizzly bears, lizards, snakes, and birds. The weather is very hot and it doesn't seem like almost autumn. There are no red or orange leaves. In fact, except for the needles of the evergreens, there are almost no leaves at all. Mr. Scatter says California trees lose their leaves early because summer is so dry and hot. I think they have all fallen off and blown to Massachusetts. That is what I would like to do.

There is no school and no lending library, no bank, no church, no meetinghouse, no newspaper, no shopping or parties or picnics, no eggs, no milk, and, worst of all, no Gram and Grampop. I miss you very much, Gram's hugs and Indian pudding with fresh cream, Grampop's laugh like a locomotive starting up. I could come home and live with you, couldn't I, and sleep in the room where Mama grew up? Please write and say yes.

I am now twelve. Yesterday was my birthday but no one remembered, not even me.

> Your loving granddaughter,
> California Morning Whipple,
> formerly of Buttonfields,
> Massachusetts, and now an
> involuntary citizen of
> Lucky Diggins, California

CHAPTER TWO

SUMMER 1849

In which we settle in and I decide to change my name

The day was hot and still, and I was hiding from Mama, which was not easy to do in a place that was just two tents lashed together. Finally I ran outside to the privy, small and cramped and smelling something awful in the hot sun, but it was private.

Sitting on the splintery plank seat, I cried from homesickness and desperate longing for Pa, for Golden buried in the Massachusetts dirt, for Gramma Whipple dead last year and Grandpa Whipple gone before I ever knew him, for the reluctant Rocky Flat dragged away by Mr. Thatcher, for Gram and Grampop, whom I could still see waving red handkerchiefs as the ship pulled out of Boston

Harbor. I had yet to mourn for picket fences and ice cream socials and the very thought of living in this unfamiliar, unloved, intolerable wilderness, when I heard Mama.

"California, where the Sam Hill have you got to? California!"

I could see her feet under the privy door and held my breath until they had passed. California: What an unfortunate name. No one in any book I ever read was called California. I never paid much attention to my name back home, because there it was just a name, like Patience or Angus or Etta Mae. But in California it was not just a name. It was a place, a passion, a promise. It was a name that caused people to notice me, talk to me, remember and expect things. It was in no way the right name for me.

So I sat back on the privy seat, put my feet up on the door, and searched my mind for a new name. I tried and discarded Rosamund, Louisa, and Desdemona before I settled on Lucy, from Mr. Abbott's "Cousin Lucy" books, which were a bit too preachy for me but were there when I had read everything else in the lending library in the basement of the Buttonfields church. I decided to call myself Lucy because it was not beautiful but ordinary, because it meant nothing but Lucy. Let some Californian be called California; I would be Lucy. It was a very Massachusetts name.

I knew I didn't fit in Lucky Diggins and I never

would. I was no rough, dirty Californian. I was a child of rich green fields and soft Thanksgiving snowfalls, of two-story houses and churches with steeples, of dairies and bake shops and stores, a gentlewoman from the east dragged all unwilling to the wilds of the west. "I am," I called proudly to a fly on the privy door, "a New Englander, with a history and culture and accomplishments!"

The door rattled. "California! Is that you? Come out of there this minute!" I opened the door and got pulled by my apron strings back into the tents that were supposed to be home now.

We passed through the front tent, with its table and benches and, behind blankets hung from the tent poles, a bed for Mama and Prairie, a mat for Butte, and the trundle I shared with Sierra and the occasional tree frog or legless lizard Butte would put beneath my quilt to devil me, into the big tent in the rear, full of bunks and boxes and chamberpots for the coming boarders. There Mama put me to work, weaving rawhide strips on wood frames for mattresses and stuffing pillow slips with cornhusks and brush.

Day followed day with no change—except for the arrival of the cookstove ($11.69 plus delivery charge) Bean Belly Thompson loaded over the mountains and down the ravine—until one morning a strange face appeared at the tent flap, a face with more hair on it than most people have on their whole head.

"Morning, sis. My tent has been invaded by a tarantula big as a chicken, so I've come to get me a bed. I ain't much for spiders. Name's Jimmy. Folk call me Jimmy Whiskers. Reckon you can tell why." Jimmy Whiskers stroked his beard and smiled the biggest smile I had seen since Pa's. His two front teeth were missing.

"We've got mice, gophers, and bugs," I said.

"As long as they ain't spiders," said Jimmy.

Mama settled with Jimmy Whiskers, who was a giant of a man. He planned to stay through the long, warm autumn and even longer if he was lucky. "I aim to find enough gold to make golden teeth for these here empty gums," he said.

Then Amos Frogge, all bones and bushy eyebrows, who had come from Texas to be a blacksmith and was building a shed out behind the general store, moved in. And the scowling Mr. Coogan, sunken eyed, scar faced, pinch mouthed, and as friendly as a thunderstorm.

I mourned my privacy and longed to have just my family about, but when I tried to tell Mama, it didn't come out right.

"Mama, do we have to have all these strangers living here? I don't . . ."

Mama narrowed her eyes and tightened her lips.

"I mean they're rough and dirty and, well, strangers."

"Get to know them," Mama said, "and they won't be strangers."

"But I don't know how to talk to them—"

"What do you mean? I've heard you babble like a brook."

"But Mama, it's different with family. You and Butte and Prairie and Sierra and Gram and Grampop and everyone, all family. These strange men . . ."

". . . pay our keep," Mama interrupted. "Now go beat biscuits for supper."

Only in the early afternoon, when the babies were sleeping, and Butte was off hunting, and Mama was kneading dough and humming "Ol' Dan Tucker," and the prospectors were off at the river washing for gold, was I able to escape, be by myself, and hide in a book. The one book I owned was *Ivanhoe,* won in a school spelling bee. I'd gotten mighty tired of it during the months of travel, but the only other thing around to read was a broadside posted on the general store about titter worm in horses.

Fortunately Massachusetts had been bursting with books, and all those I had ever read were still there in my head. So one day, good and sick of *Ivanhoe,* I leaned back against the taut canvas of the tent, closed my eyes, and found a way to leave Lucky Diggins. I became the beauteous Madeline following her lover through icy corridors in "The Eve of St. Agnes" and imagined the lava pouring over my body during the last days of

Pompeii. I took on the elegance and culture of Queen Elizabeth and Juliet and Maria Edgeworth's ladies: "Lord Rackrent, how excruciatingly delightful to see you," I murmured to the tent pole and sighed lavishly.

Looking up, I saw Prairie—almost seven, short and round, big eyes even bigger behind her wire-rimmed spectacles, and nearly the whole of one grubby hand in her mouth, fiddling with a loose front tooth.

Prairie mumbled something.

"Take your hand out of your mouth and say it again," I told her.

"What are you doing?"

"Never mind. What do you want?"

"Mama said you would help me find a place for a garden."

"You can't plant a garden until spring. Why do we have to find it now?"

"The soil must be got ready, of course, if things are to grow right." Prairie loved growing things. Grampop always said Prairie was like him—just tickled the ground and it laughed beans.

Dear Gram and Grampop,

Please do not address yours truly as California anymore, California Morning Whipple being a foolish name for a duck much less a girl. I call myself Lucy now. I cannot hate California and be California. I know you will understand.

13

I miss you so much. A prospector who slept here one night had two mules, which I had to feed. I called them Gram and Grampop. The lady mule was gray like Gram and the other laughed just like Grampop.

> *With much love from your*
> *granddaughter,*
> *Lucy Whipple*

CHAPTER THREE

AUTUMN 1849

*In which Mama tries to make me a mighty hunter
and I finally get hungry enough to shoot*

"If you want to eat, missy, you are going to have to
find a way to put food on this table," said Mama,
sweeping at my feet with her broom.

Lord-a-mercy, I thought, fixing Mama with my
fiercest glare. Don't I do enough what with helping to
cook and wash for all those hairy strangers in the bunks
in the back tent? Don't I teach Prairie her letters, her
numbers, and a little about the history of Massachusetts
each morning? Isn't that enough?

"Not nearly enough," said Mama, as if reading my
mind. She snatched *Ivanhoe* from my hands and tossed
it into the soapy water of the laundry tub. With a yelp

I fished it out and spread it in the sunshine to dry. I expected it would soon be as good as new except for some wrinkled pages, but I decided I'd better take Mama seriously.

"What do you want me to do, Mama?"

"Take this shotgun and shoot us some rabbits or a squirrel."

"But Mama, I can't go shooting little animals!" I didn't relish the idea of shooting living things. I was much too sensitive, and the powder would make my hands stink.

"Don't Mama me. What do you think stew is? And bacon? Meat. From animals. Butte can't hunt, now he has his job with Mr. Scatter, so you will have to do it." Butte was sweeping and stacking at the general store and had started calling himself the man of the family, until Mama grabbed his nose and said, "No, you ain't the man of this family. There is no man in this family, only a lady and some little children, and that will have to do." Didn't keep him from swaggering and counting his pay in front of me before he gave it to Mama. For all he was just ten, almost two years younger than me, Butte sure could lord it up.

"Couldn't we just buy meat from the store?"

"One, Mr. Scatter doesn't get much meat. Two, what he does get is too darned expensive. Three, I have a perfectly able daughter with a perfectly good trigger finger."

"Prairie doesn't do anything but watch Sierra and pull weeds. She could hunt."

"Prairie is only six. It will have to be you. I can't feed three hungry boarders and the five of us on beans and the bits of salt pork and dried beef Bean Belly Thompson hauls in from Sacramento every few weeks. Now go."

Mama shoved the shotgun into my hands and pushed me out the door quick as a cat.

My pa had taught me and Butte to shoot back home, but I never took to it, preferring a book any day to the jolt and noise and smell of shooting. Now Pa was dead and we had come west and Mama was trying to make a westerner out of me.

The first morning I sat on a stump outside the tent and fretted. The place was so wild, just trees and hills and tents. I could almost see wild Indians coming up the Sacramento River to the Yuba and up the Yuba to the Forks and on to Lucky Diggins, right to where I sat on the stump with a gun in my lap.

Near noon I saw a movement in the dry grass. It looked like feathers. Indians! I bolted into the tent.

"I had to come back, Mama," I said. "I saw feathers and . . ."

"I know, I know," said Mama. "They were wild Indians and you were in imminent danger of being captured and living the rest of your life on acorns and roasted grasshoppers."

"But Mama . . ."

"But Mama nothing. That was most likely a wild turkey you let get away." Mama sighed. "Go feed Prairie and Sierra."

That night we had no meat for supper. I, in fact, had no supper at all and wouldn't, so Mama said, until I brought home something to eat.

I watched the rest eat their beans and biscuits. "If I were with Gram," I muttered, "I would be eating chicken from Larrabee's farm or store-bought bacon."

Mama said nothing.

The second day I sat three hours on the tree stump with the gun in my lap, imagining myself as the dashing Ivanhoe's secret love, as beautiful as Rowena and as plucky as Rebecca but much smarter and better read.

Suddenly there was a rustling in the grass. "Mama!" I ran for the tent. "There's something out there. Sounded like a grizzly or . . ."

Mama banged the skillet down on the cookstove. "Lord, you are the spookiest child. When you were little, wind spooked you. Lantern light blinking in the window spooked you. The clown at Hallelujah Purdy's Circus and Hippodramatic Exposition spooked you." She picked up a spoon and waved it at me. "Now you're near grown up, you've gotten worse instead of better. Grizzlies! Indians! Won't shoot a gun! Want to lie around with your nose in a book! What is to become of you, girl?" Mama plopped a gob of bacon grease into

18

the skillet and shook her head. "Every tub has to learn to stand on its own bottom sometime."

I got no supper again, but I must allow that in a curious way I was proud of myself. I might starve to death, but I'd go a New Englander.

The third day I ventured off the stump. I watched a blue jay gather buckeyes from a tree overhanging the ravine, followed a lizard as it skittled from sunny spot to sunny spot, made shadow pictures of a fox, a duck, and a swan on the canvas of the tent. And I went to visit Sweetheart, the old mean and ugly mule with one brown and one white ear who had brought us to Lucky Diggins.

Sweetheart lived behind the tent in a shelter Butte and I had made of canvas draped over a framework of tree branches. Missing Rocky Flat, the barn cats, and Gram's canaries, we tried to love Sweetheart. For the mule's part, she'd as soon bite. And she did. I rubbed the red spot on my arm that would soon turn into a bruise and returned to the stump.

Finally, hungry and afraid to push Mama any further, I closed my eyes, pulled the trigger a few times, and, lo and behold, shot a squirrel. It was blasted near to pieces and no good for anyone to eat except a dog or a coyote but I took it into the tent, dropped it on the table, and lay down on my bed to read *Ivanhoe*.

"I plan to rent out your bed," said Mama, "to someone who will pay for it. Kindly remove your carcass."

At that I realized Mama's stubborn streak was a mile wider and a good deal deeper than mine. I sat outside the cabin day after day shooting rabbits and squirrels and any wild creature that moved until I discovered that I didn't mind killing birds as much, so we ate prairie chicken every day and would, I said, until someone else agreed to do the hunting. Jimmy Whiskers said prairie chicken with biscuits and lard gravy didn't taste bad at all, but the buckshot sure was hard on his gums.

Mr. Coogan said nothing but looked at me as though I were a hog and he a butcher. I had a bad feeling about that man.

Dear Gram and Grampop,

More boarders have moved in, but we are far from full and won't be until spring. Amos Frogge says some miners are thieves and drunkards, men of bad habits and worse dispositions; others can be counted as the finest folk on God's green earth. I'm sick of them all—dirty boots and dirty sheets, loud voices and big appetites.

We have to eat supper with them every night. Mr. Coogan near ruins it for me with his scowling and muttering and all-around bad nature. He isn't a miner like Jimmy or a blacksmith like Amos. I don't know what he does or is—except mean. He smacked Prairie once for spilling coffee on some papers he had, and Mama didn't even say a word to him.

If we didn't have the only boarding house in town,

Mama would be even more worried about business than she already is. Her cooking is no worse than it was at home, but her baking is so bad that I have, in desperation, taken it over, except that Mama still makes the bread. She claims I get too dreamy while kneading. Butte and the babies and I are used to Mama's hard, dry bread, but we don't have to pay for it. The boarders haven't complained much though, even Mr. Coogan. And they eat as if it were fancy cooking sent us by the Vanderbilts in New York.

Jimmy Whiskers has built me a shelf next to my bed. It kind of wobbles, but I put on it stacks of my aprons and stockings, a shell from the Massachusetts shore, my copy of Ivanhoe, *and an empty herring tub where I plan to keep your letters, when they come. Jimmy says writing letters is like tossing words to the wind, for the mail takes three months or more to get all the way to Massachusetts and three months or so to get back here, if it doesn't get stolen by outlaws, lost in a landslide, or sunk to the bottom of the sea. He says writing letters is an act of faith.*

Except for letters, I'm not strong on faith these days. I had faith Pa would always be with me and he died. I had faith that I'd be safe at home and here I am stuck in this wilderness. I suspect I'm about out of faith.

Love to you both from your
granddaughter,
Lucy Whipple

With the heat of the day and the blazing of the cookstove, the tent stayed hot as the Bad Place until well after dark. Finally I got out of bed and went outside in search of a breeze. The sky was full of stars. They looked almost like fireflies, but you can't catch them in your hands. I knew better than even to try.

CHAPTER FOUR

AUTUMN 1849

*In which I remember Pa, tell Prairie,
and find some comfort therein*

"Call me Lucy," I finally said to Prairie.

"Mmph?" said Prairie. I pulled her hand from her mouth. "Why?" Prairie said again.

"I want it to be my name."

"Why?"

"I don't like California."

"Why?"

"It doesn't suit me—neither the name nor the place."

"Why?"

"Tarnation! I swear if you ask me why one more time I'll chop you up and feed you to the lizards."

"Wh—"

I shoved Prairie's hand back into her mouth. "Mercy! Mercy! Ask me anything but no more *why*."

"Why not?" Prairie fairly gleamed at her own cleverness. "All right, all right. Then answer this: What did our pa look like? Did he look like me?" Prairie was too young to remember him well.

I didn't much like talking about Pa, for it made me miss him terrible instead of just ordinary bad. Sometimes when a longing for Pa would get so big it was hurtful, I'd close my eyes and press the hog-bristle scrub brush to my cheek and pretend it was his red and scratchy beard and that he was not buried in the Massachusetts ground at all but was holding me on his lap, singing about California Morning to the tune of "The Holly and the Ivy," the way he did when I couldn't sleep.

"Well," I said this time, "you have blue eyes, like he did, not no-color like mine. But you are little and plump and run around like a steam engine. Pa was the skinniest man I ever saw. He had red hair and a big laugh, and he liked nothing better than just lying in the fields looking up at the sky."

Pa had been a reluctant shopkeeper, inheritor of a stable and feed store from his own dead pa, and dreamer of dreams about better things—new places, big land, out west, toward the setting sun.

"On Sundays," I told Prairie, surprised to find a bit of comfort in the remembering, "he wouldn't put on his overalls. He would take clean woolen pants kept under the mattress to press them, and wear a clean shirt Mama had ironed with the heavy flatiron and his best coat and the paisley scarf he got in Boston. Sundays, when he could escape Gramma Whipple's eye, he wouldn't go to church at all but into the world beyond the town, often toting me along with him."

Sometimes we walked in the woods, I told Prairie, other times rode on Pa's horse to Oakbridge and ate cold meat and apples on the village green, and in winter took the sleigh through the frozen fields, holding hot potatoes in our gloved hands to keep them warm. Once I asked Pa where the water from the creek went, so we followed it to the stream and then to the river and all the way to the sea. I was frightened by the noise and the vastness of the water but, as always, putting my hand into Pa's big brown one made me feel safe.

The last Sunday in the October before we left Massachusetts, Pa and I walked in the woods to see the changing leaves, and he talked again about moving west. Word of the gold lying in the California streets and fields had reached Buttonfields, and Pa and Mama were more anxious than ever to go.

"Gramma Whipple used to say it is wicked to want more than you have," I told Pa. "She said we should just stay put and thank God."

"Your Gramma Whipple was a scared old lady with a hard life, California. Doesn't mean *you* should be scared of new things. Change is coming. It's in the air. People are opening their eyes and looking around and seeing there's more to this world than stables and fields and the general store."

"I like the general store."

He waved his hand. "I mean there is a whole world out there, and we are going to get us some. Just think, California, of the mountains and deserts and vast unknown places we'll see. It will be quite a change from this dull Massachusetts town."

"I like things the way they are."

"I know, but everything changes."

"Why do they, Pa? Seems I just get used to green leaves when they turn red, just start liking red leaves when they fall. Or I just get used to baby Sierra and she's up and walking. Or people start moving away and places change. Why can't life just stay the way it is?"

"Life changes. That's the way of it. This old Greek fellow Heraclitus said there is nothing permanent except change, and I reckon he was right."

I don't know where my pa got his information. He'd had no schooling since he was twelve, and we owned no books except my *Ivanhoe*, but he knew all sorts of things. I didn't care if they were true or not; I believed them all.

As we walked, he pointed out objects to me as he always did—birds' eggs, a snakeskin, bits of pottery and flint chips from the Indians who'd lived there before.

"Look," he'd say, "look, California." Mama always said *look* was Pa's favorite word; it meant admire, wonder, goggle at the beauty and excitement all around us. I'd look at whatever it was and pick it up and lock it away in the wooden box I called my treasure chest.

That Sunday he said, "Look," and there was a woodpecker tap-tap-tapping at a fallen log right in front of us. The tapping was so loud the bird did not hear us approach, and Pa reached right out with his big gentle hands and grabbed it. He calmed it by stroking its red feathered head and then brought it close so I could feel the beating of its heart beneath the softness of its feathers. The bird looked right at me, eyes bright in a black eye mask, so it seemed very like a tiny bandit in a red hat.

"Let's keep it, Pa. We could build it a cage."

"No, California, this is a wild thing."

"But it would be much safer in a cage by the house than out here in the wild."

"There are more important things than being safe, daughter," Pa said.

"Not to me," I said.

I couldn't keep the woodpecker, but I did get a red feather for my treasure chest. I couldn't keep my pa either. Three weeks later he was dead of pneumonia and the baby Golden with him. They were buried together so that only one hole would have to be dug in the frozen ground.

I think Golden must have liked that. I would have if it were me, snuggled up against Pa's side with my cheek against his hog-bristle–scrub-brush–like red beard. I put my treasure chest in with them. And there they all are to this day.

Dear Gram and Grampop,

It is odd to think you will not get this letter until after Christmas. Butte thinks it silly of me to write, but it makes me feel closer to you.

If I were home right now, Gram and I would be making squash pies and pear butter and stringing apple slices to dry before the fire, and the air would be heavy with their tangy smell. Butte would be out early to check the size of the pumpkins and likely drop a big load of dry leaves on Prairie and Sierra, who would laugh.

Instead we are here in California, working too hard and doing none of those things, and it is hot, and I am a stranger in a land where they even speak a different language, full of derns *and* dings *and have you a pickaxe about your clothes? The prospectors frighten me, being so loud and dirty, as well as the rowdiest bunch I ever did see, fighting and cussing and getting drunk as ducks, liquor being cheaper than food. One night we heard gunshots and looked out to find that someone had shot out the lanterns in the saloon and run off with all the gambling money. I was wishing Pa was here, but he's not and I am. I am bodaciously sorrow-burdened and wretched!*

CHAPTER FIVE

AUTUMN 1849

*In which I go into the pie business,
and Butte is overtaken by gold fever*

Early nearly every day I mixed and patted and rolled crusts for pies. I sprinkled sugar on them, pricked the crusts in swirling designs with the prongs of a fork, admired my artistry, and baked them for supper. Fresh apple was my favorite, but we didn't have fresh apples. We had to settle for dried-apple and, sometimes, even vinegar pie, just vinegar and sugar, with the only apples supplied by our imaginations.

One fine morning I took a fistful of dried apples to munch on and went out and sat on the stump until my bottom grew sore, trying to come up with a way to get back home to Massachusetts. Here I was in gold country with fortunes being dug out of the ground. If I could figure out how to divert some of it my way, I had shot my last squirrel, surprised my last lizard, boiled my last sheet, seen my last min—

"Pardon me, little sister, might you have some water about you?"

Standing there was a miner, booted and flannel shirted and very dirty. In my imagination already back in Massachusetts, I just sat and stared at him.

Mama shouted through the tent flap, "Get off that stump and dip some water for the poor man, you goose."

I took the tin cup hanging from a string on the tent, dipped it into the rain barrel, which had more leaves in it than water, and gave it to the miner.

He drank thirstily and handed me back the cup. "Thank you entirely for the water, little sister. Now maybe you could tell me what smells so durned good."

"The dried-apple pies I made for supper," I said.

"I think I might trade this whole bag of gold here for one of them pies."

"Done," I said.

The miner laughed. We settled on a bit of gold dust and I gave him a pie.

"California, there must be ten dollars worth of gold here," Mama said. "For one pie!"

The gold dust inspired me to bake another couple of pies. I sat on the stump with pies cooling beside me all afternoon, but lucky miners were rare, and lucky miners who would spend their dust on pies when the saloon was nearby were rarer still.

"The secret," said Amos Frogge, who stopped by to sniff but didn't buy because he got pie free with his supper, "is to get them before they head to the saloon."

So the next morning I got out of bed long before dawn to do my chores and bake my pies. I gathered enough chokecherries for six pies, put them in to bake, built a carrier out of the old straw basket we had come west with, and, not long after sunup, set out for the river to make my fortune. I didn't much relish the thought of talking all those strangers into buying pies, but I thought I could manage if it would get me away from this dirt pile called Lucky Diggins.

I sold my first pie to a man and his scrawny wife who were passing through. I got a dollar, and that lady just stood there, leaning on the mule, and ate the whole pie, washing it down with cold river water.

Pies two and three were bought by Jimmy Whiskers. It was late morning before pie four went to a group digging near the north bank.

I began to worry about getting home to help Mama clean up from breakfast, feed Prairie and Sierra, and begin peeling and slicing and boiling for dinner. As I walked back along the north bank, I saw a stranger wearing not a flannel shirt and boots like most diggers but just a red union suit and a straw hat. Most peculiar, but I approached him. "Mister, could I int—"

"Dag diggety!" shouted the miner in his underwear.
"Git yer carcass off'n my claim afore I bury my shovel
in yer yella hair, you diggety dog. Spyin' on me! Waitin'
to jump my claim and steal my gold, you diggety . . ."
The miner continued mumbling while he pulled a pistol from the seat of his union suit and fired it in my
direction.

Horror! Bullets were hitting the ground all around
my feet, so I dropped the basket of pies and took off for
home, scrambling over the ground like a blind chicken
with the fidgets. The remaining pies were eaten by a
badger, who then curled up inside the basket to sleep
and nearly scared me to death when I went back the
next morning, causing me to holler so loud that the
badger took off toward the mountains and is likely running still.

Two things came of this encounter. "Dag diggety"
began to creep into my vocabulary, especially on those
occasions when the little girls were ill-humored or I was
feeling unappreciated, though I never dared to let
Mama hear it, lest it be judged blasphemous and for-
bidden. Second, I decided that a one-person pie business was too hard, too time-consuming, and just too
dangerous, so I looked around for a partner.

Of course. Butte.

I called him to a business meeting out by the stump.
"Listen, Butte, it's a great opportunity," I told him,
feeding him bits of dried apple to keep him from wan-

dering off. "I will make the pies, and you take them out to the river and the diggings and sell them. You'll earn a nickel for each pie you sell."

"Nope."

"Well, then, ten cents a pie. That's ten percent and it could add up to a lot of money. Why, there must be a thousand miners within a day's walk of here. If even half of them bought a pie, that would be five hundred dollars. Just think of it, Butte, five hundred dollars! A couple of weeks like that and we'd be on our way back to Massachusetts."

"Massachusetts? Why'd I want to go back there?"

"Surely you don't want to stay in this hot, dusty wilderness?"

"I like it here."

We had gotten off the original subject. "Well, stay then. I'll take the five hundred dollars and go home."

"Good. Be sure to write."

"All right, I yield. Fifteen percent."

"Twenty."

"You're joking!"

"Twenty-five."

"Listen, Butte, I—"

"Thirty, and give my share to Mama."

"Done," I said in a hurry. Dag diggety, I thought, if we don't cease negotiations, I'll see no profit at all.

So Butte and I became partners in the pie business. Mr. Scatter let Butte go early on Tuesdays and

Saturdays, so on those days I baked and he peddled pies up and down the river. Mr. Scatter gave us an old cracked pickle crock to keep our earnings in.

I dreamed of making my fortune and getting home by next spring, but it seemed as though the more money we made, the more I had to pay to Mr. Scatter for flour and lard, and the more Mama took to keep us all in boots and beans and bad coffee. Everything had to be carted over the mountains by Bean Belly Thompson or someone like him, so prices were monstrously high. Apples and onions were two dollars each, beans a dollar a pound, and Mr. Scatter had a can of pickled beets on his shelf priced at eleven dollars, waiting for the right lucky miner who wanted to celebrate with pickled beets.

Not too many miners made their fortunes either, and every week one or two boarders would leave to go back to farm or factory, a mite scrawnier but no richer than when they came. Every week one or two more young fellows would take their place, hopes running high. They came with picks and axes and tin pans, with lucky charms and holy medals, with magic machines called Goldometers and Nugget Finders, with secret maps and Indian legends. Few planned to stay in California after they made their fortunes, so there was no planting of crops, raising of cattle or pigs, or building of anything but the crudest temporary shelter. They just wanted to get rich, get out, and get home.

Some were lucky, most were not. The work was hard and full of danger. Some died before ever putting pick to dirt, worn out by the long months of crossing the country, living on salt beef and stale biscuits. Jimmy Whiskers said those who stayed on were more greedy, more needy, more stubborn, or more hopeful than the rest or, like him, just had nowhere else to go.

Tramping out to the goldfields every Tuesday and Saturday made Butte vulnerable to a bad case of gold fever. He started spending more and more time out at the diggings, even when he didn't have pies to sell, and at home he could only think gold and talk gold.

"Listen, California . . ." he said one day.

"Call me Lucy, will you?"

"Why'd I want to do that?"

"Because I want it to be my name."

"Lucy? Makes you sound like some dainty showoff from the city. Lucy Belle. Lucy May. Lucy dearest." He snickered.

"Never mind. What do you want?"

"Want out of the pie business. Between working with the miners and cleaning up for Mr. Scatter, there's no time for pies."

"You can't just quit. You're a partner," I grumbled. "You can't. I barely have time to make the pies; I'd never finish all my work around here if I had to sell, too. I'll give you an extra five percent."

"No matter. I give it all to Mama anyway."

So Butte quit, leaving me to try to keep the business going all by myself. Mama grumbled about having to do without Butte's profits, but she was the first one to understand itchy feet, so she let him have his adventure. He went out early every day but Sunday, when Mama made him stay home and take a bath. Otherwise he spent his mornings working for Mr. Scatter, sweeping, stacking boxes, emptying spittoons, and shoveling the mule droppings away from the saloon door. His days went to digging holes and carrying water and tending mules for the men who shoveled tons of dirt and gravel into the long cradles, hoping there were chunks of gold that would get caught in the riffles in the bottom and make their fortunes. He picked up tools, patched up cuts and bruises, and learned to fight. He was paid with bits of dust when his miners got lucky and a pat on the back when they didn't. Mostly he just came home with sore arms and a story to tell.

"Heard tell of a prospector out Coyote Gulch who decided to turn tail and go home, his partner dying on him and no luck washing for color. So he burns his gear, digs a grave for his partner, and there in the hole turns up the biggest nugget ever seen in these parts. Living now in San Francisco, lightin' his cigars with dollar bills, not likely ever to go home. Seems to me there's no point in workin' steady if, with a little luck and a sharp pick, you can find fortunes lyin' on the ground."

He took to swaggering and spitting and asking me

every day if he had started a beard yet. He made the mistake of spitting where Mama could see him, and she frowned mightily. I wondered how much longer he'd be working in the diggings.

Butte slept soundly each night, worn out from being a little boy doing a man's job. Sometimes when I was up late into the night baking pies, I watched him sleep, his eyelashes making half-circles on his cheeks and his breath whistling in the silence of the night, and tried to figure out just how I felt about him, he vexed me so. It was a long time before I knew.

CHAPTER SIX

Autumn/Winter 1849–1850

*In which I try to tell Mama my name, write letters,
and threaten to sigh myself to death*

I finally got up the courage to approach Mama about this Lucy matter. "Mama, can I ask you something?"

"Depends on what," said Mama as she poured molasses and mustard powder into the pot of beans.

"Will you . . . umm . . ." I didn't quite know how to make Mama see that this was important to me and not joke or snort in irritation.

"Spit it out, California." Mama stirred the beans once more and put them into the oven of the cookstove.

"That's it, Mama. California. I don't want to be called California. California is a place, not a person. I want to be called Lucy."

38

Mama stopped in the middle of licking the molasses spoon. "What are you talking about?"

I could feel my cheeks grow hot as the cookstove. "About me, Mama. I want to be called Lucy, not California."

"Lucy? Where did you come up with a name like that?"

"In a book. But it doesn't matter—"

"A book! I should have known. That's what makes you so notional, those books!"

"Mama, please!"

Mama looked at me twisting my hands in my apron and trying hard not to cry. She sighed. "After twelve years of calling you California, I don't see how I can suddenly say Lucy any more than I could Bossie or Nelly or Lady Jane."

"Will you try, Mama?"

"We'll see. Now go do something useful."

I straightened my apron and took a deep breath. "I will go write some letters."

"You will gather wood for the cookstove, beat the dust out of the bed quilts, put the sheets on to boil, rub salt and vinegar into the ink stains on your aprons and lay them in the sun, and set the table for supper. Then you can write some letters," said Mama, and that was that.

Dear Gram and Grampop,

Well, I told Mama about me being Lucy instead of California, and now she just calls me missy or chickie or sis or nothing at all. To her I'm not Lucy yet but I'm not California either, and that sits just fine with me. If I were the gambling sort, I'd bet a penny she will call me Lucy before too long. I think she'd be embarrassed to stand outside the tent and shout, "Oh chickie, come home and start supper." I will keep you informed.

I liked writing letters. There wasn't much else to do for fun in Lucky Diggins if you didn't dig or drink. At first I wrote on pink writing paper, a going-away gift from Aunt Beulah, but was finally reduced to using the scraps of greasy paper that came wrapped around the bacon and cheese and lard from Mr. Scatter's store.

Dear Cousin Batty,

Do not let your father bring you here, for you would not like it and would most likely die. At the least you would get your hands dirty and mud on your pretty white shoes.

I do not like it, and I do not mind mud nearly as much as you do.

It is lonely here. I even almost miss you.

> *Regards from your cousin who*
> *now calls herself*
> *Lucy*

It was a lot easier to write what I thought or felt than to say it out loud. I could write things I'd never say to someone's face, especially since I didn't quite believe those letters would ever get all the way around to Massachusetts. Snowshoe Ballou, who had the biggest feet in the Sierra, carried letters to San Francisco for mailing and brought mail back, for a dollar a letter. He walked up and down the mountains and valleys, on a trail when there was a trail or navigating by trees and peaks or stars when there wasn't. Lucky Diggins was all in a dither each month when Snowshoe Ballou showed up, bringing the promise of a letter or newspaper or a package from some faraway exotic place or, even better, from home.

Dear Gram and Grampop,

If ever you write, please enclose money so I can pay Snowshoe Ballou and continue to write you letters. Gold would be best, but I believe dollars would do.

I am still selling a few pies, so I have been making a little money each day for my pickle crock, but most of the miners don't seem to care for pie much, preferring to spend their money on beans, whiskey, and tobacco. Mr. Scatter says all miners are vagabonds, scoundrels, and assassins, but that he's not leaving until he has "enough money to burn a wet mule." The miners, on the other hand, think Mr. Scatter is the scoundrel, taking all their precious gold to pay for flour and salt. "Hard as Scatter's heart" is heard around here near as often as "pay dirt," "humbug," and "more whiskey, dang it."

Snowshoe Ballou was my first real friend in

California. He had a sweet smile and appreciated a slice or two of pie whenever he picked up letters. I didn't even know we were friends until his third or fourth visit, when he brought me an eagle feather, for he didn't talk much. I don't know if he got used to silence because of being alone in the mountains or if he took to the mountains because they were silent. And he never said.

Dear Gram and Grampop,

Mama said that we are all fine and healthy and if I cannot write nicer things than I usually do, I cannot write at all. Expect to hear only good things from now on, whether they are true or not. You'll begin to think Lucky Diggins is as calm as a toad in the sunshine.

Snowshoe's best friend was an Indian called Hennit, which meant Beaver, for his thick brown hair. Jimmy Whiskers told me Snowshoe and Hennit would sit in the big Indian sweathouse for hours, cleaning themselves of all human smell, and then go hunting for the deer Snowshoe used for making his shoes, his feet being too big for ready-mades. After hunting, Jimmy said, Snowshoe and Hennit would thank the spirit of the deer for sharing his hide and his meat with them. I thought it was a good idea and for a while thanked the prairie chickens and rabbits and squirrels I shot, but it never seemed quite enough.

Dear Gram and Grampop,

I dreamed last night of clam chowder and Gram's apple pandowdy with sweet yellow cream. Woke to a bean-and-biscuit breakfast again. We eat lots of beans and biscuits. Except for what I shoot, our meat is mostly the weevils in the flour or some moldy salt pork that traveled halfway around the world to find us and did not have an easy trip. I think such a diet cannot be as healthy for little children as wholesome Massachusetts food, but when I try to talk to Mama of this, she looks like she's going to spit.

If you see my former teacher, Miss Charlotte Homer of Reedsville, kindly inquire if she might send me a book. I am sick to death of Ivanhoe *and Mr. Scatter's Bible, and there is not another book in these mountains.*

Once when Snowshoe seemed more talkative than usual, I asked him why he took to the mountains and the mails. Snowshoe shrugged and said, "Know many, trust few, always paddle your own canoe."

"Don't you have family?" I asked.

Snowshoe said he didn't recollect.

Dear Gram and Grampop,

You would not know me. I am so tall and almost fat. I think it is all the biscuits and gravy. I do the biscuits but Mama makes fine gravy. It is one reason her boarding house is full, that and the fact the miners like to look at her, her being the only woman in the camp except for

Milly, who has come to work at the saloon, and Mr.
Scatter's grown daughter, Belle, who has cross-eyes and
bad skin and is as mean as a meat axe. Maybe she should
marry Mr. Coogan and they can go into the meanness busi-
ness: two bits a frown, a dollar a scowl, and a twenty-
dollar gold piece would buy you flat-out savagerous rage.

Mr. Scatter has hired Snoose McGrath to build an honest-
to-gosh wooden boarding house behind the general store, so
we are hoping to be out of this tent by winter. Mama works
hard but sees only the mountains and big trees and clear
blue sky and doesn't seem to see the dirt. I myself am knee
deep in dirt.

I am getting more used to boarders and even open my
mouth now and then, but it seems just as I'm getting
friendly, they leave, going home or to the city for the win-
ter, except for Mr. Coogan, who gives every indication of
becoming a permanent member of the Whipple family.

We look never to get out of here. My heart is so sore
with missing you and Pa and Golden and home, sometimes
I think I'll sigh myself to death.

I asked Jimmy why Snowshoe kept so quiet and alone
all the time.

"He ain't much for other people," Jimmy said.

"Doesn't he have any kin?"

"Well," said Jimmy, scratching his beard with his
fork, "there's Hennit, though I don't suppose you'd
exactly call him kin. And there was the duck."

"What duck?"

"Old Snowshoe used to own a killer duck named Goliath. He would take that duck from mining camp to mining camp to fight with dogs and make a lot of money on. Seems no one would bet on a duck against a dog, but no dog could beat that duck. Except one." Jimmy sighed. "Guess you'd have to say that duck was like Snowshoe's kin."

Dear Uncle Matt, Aunt Beulah, and Cousin Batty,

We just received the letter you sent us last summer. It was the first we've gotten here in Lucky Diggins, and what a pleasure to hear from you and know all that little Batty is doing. I am sure she deserved the spelling prize and the art medal, and we are all pulling for her to be Easter Princess, you can just imagine.

Mama and I keep very busy with the boarding house, washing dirty sheets and skinning rabbits and boiling bear fat and lye for soap. Butte still fetches and carries for miners and rents our mule, Sweetheart, for a dollar a day to new-comers who need help lugging their belongings upriver. Butte also works mornings sweeping out the saloon. The more the miners drink, the more gold dust gets dropped on the floor, so he has taken to sifting the sweepings. He found enough last week to pay for a barrel of salted beef that was only part rotted, and we have enjoyed it for supper ever since.

Prairie takes care of Sierra and pulls weeds and is right now spreading manure on what will be our vegetable patch next summer. Sierra only toddles and messes in her diapers, but we expect that for she is only two. I think we should just let Sierra sit in the vegetable patch to save labor.

Mama found this letter before it was mailed, and that was the end of my letter writing for a while. She made me take over Prairie's job of gathering mule manure for the garden. This is how I learned that writing can be dangerous as grizzlies if it falls into the wrong hands.

Dear Gram and Grampop,

It is almost Christmas. If you would like to know what presents I would like, well, they are a book and a dress with cabbage roses, although I am not hinting, for I know you will not even get this letter by Christmas.

As Christmas came closer, the boarding house was filled with whisperings, secrets, and giggles as we made presents for one another: rosehip necklaces, corncob dolls, taffy, and molasses popcorn balls. On Christmas Eve, while darning Snowshoe's stockings as a present for him, I lamented over a Christmas without turkey and mince pies, eggnog and sleigh rides, Gram and Grampop. Then I thought of the man with big feet crossing the pass in the snow with no kin but a dead duck. I went and hugged Mama, Prairie, Sierra, and even Butte, who grumbled but did not shove me away.

46

Dear Gram and Grampop,

Thank you for The Little Christian's Book of Pious Thoughts *that you sent me for Christmas. Imagine my surprise when I opened my Christmas package and there it was.*

I hope you will like the pressed-flower picture I sent you. Jimmy Whiskers said the flowers are from the manzanita tree, which does not grow in Massachusetts but thrives in California because it can spread out.

I know you are right, that Mama needs me here to help, but I am sorry you think me too much trouble to offer a room to. You are not that old.

> *Yours very truly,*
> *Lucy Whipple*

CHAPTER SEVEN

WINTER 1850

*In which I hunt for Rattlesnake Jake
and have to eat my supper standing up*

That winter was the coldest and wettest anyone
could remember. Rain fell day after day on the tents
and trees and the blacksmith shop, on the half-built
wooden buildings and the piles of garbage in the street,
on rabbit burrows and grizzly caves, on Indians and
miners and shopkeepers, and on me.

Creeks flooded, rivers overflowed their banks, sending tents and shacks floating down to the bay and out to
sea. No one could work, no one could even walk without
losing his boots in the deep, sticky mud. Our tents grew
soaked during the day and froze in the cold each night.

Pack trains stopped altogether, and we were dependent on what we could catch or find or borrow to eat.

Sometimes I stood at the tent flap, just watching the downpour, thinking with great longing of the Massachusetts rain, not icy needles like this but big soft drops that made quarter-sized spots on the dry ground, big juicy drops we caught on our tongues and swallowed to relieve our thirst. I'd stand there until my eyelashes grew heavy with frost and one or other of the boarders would grab the tent flap from my hand, shouting, "Dang bab it, little sister, it's so cold in here, my britches is froze to my bum, pardon me altogether."

The few miners who stayed over the winter spent their days and nights at the saloon until the whiskey ran out. Then they came back to the boarding house, and we got to know one another very well, for the cold rain kept us all inside a good deal of the time, working, telling stories, arguing, and complaining.

One afternoon the rain washed in a curly-headed young man from out east who'd gotten lost on his way from Downieville. He wore the miners' boots and flannels with a high black silk hat left over from his days as a dandy. He shaved every week and never spat indoors. We called him the Gent.

The Gent was tall enough to break icicles off the tent poles to suck on, and he could play "Aura Lee" and "I Gave My Love a Penny" on his fiddle, the first music heard in Lucky Diggins that wasn't provided by mules,

jays, and the roaring of the river. Each night we huddled around the cookstove trying to keep warm and listened and sang and tapped our feet in time.

"You know," Amos said, when the Gent finished a
particularly jolly "Sweet Betsy from Pike," "there ain't
nothin' like a ballad on a rainy night."

"What do you mean, ballad?" I asked.

"Well, little sister, I'd say a ballad is a poem that tells
a story of the extraordinary doin's of ordinary folk. You
can say ballads or sing 'em or jist play their tunes for
folks who know. I learned me lots of ballads in Texas."

"Tell us one. Please."

"You jist sit back and listen, sis, and I'll tell you a good
one. Imagine we're outside, settin' round a fire of cow pies
and dry grass. But for the fire it's so dark you couldn't
find your nose with both hands, and there you sit, lookin'
at the moon through the neck of a bottle and listenin' to
the coyotes sing when someone starts in tellin':

"This here's the ballad of Rattlesnake Jake,
     A man as mean as sin.
     He used barbed wire to comb his hair
     And gargled with straight gin.

"He picked his teeth with a Bowie knife.
     He'd rob, he'd shoot, he'd kill.
     He pushed old ladies off of cliffs
     And babies down the hill."

50

"Thunderation! What a villain!" Jimmy Whiskers cried as he threw a piece of pine wood into the stove. "If I ever catch up with him . . ." The Gent shushed him, and Jimmy sat back down again, scratching his belly as he listened. Amos Frogge continued.

> "Till Sheriff Bueller came to town
> With star of shiny tin.
> Said, 'I swear on my mother's grave,
> I'm bringin' that outlaw in.'

> "So while the townfolk all raised Hell,
> No one went to jail,
> For the sheriff was busy as bees in June
> Following Rattlesnake's trail.

> "He tracked him through the mountain snow,
> And down the river he chased,
> Till in a cabin dark as death
> The two came face to face.

> "The sheriff stood in the cabin door,
> His eyes were mad and hot.
> But Jake was ready, cool as ice,
> And dropped him in one shot."

Mama had stopped sweeping and was leaning on her broom to listen, while Prairie had crawled onto my lap.

I hardly noticed, so caught up was I in the tale of the villainous Rattlesnake Jake. I had assumed this was going to be just a story, but it sounded so real, as if Jake could be down any road or behind any tree.

"The bullet went plumb through the sheriff
  As only bullets can,
  Bounced off a bedpost made of iron
  And the miner's pick and pan.

"*Clang* went a kettle when the bullet struck,
  Bouncing off with such a force
  The chimney shook, a brick fell down
  And squashed the sheriff's horse.

"The skies grew dark, the wind blew fierce,
  And the bullet, as if beguiled,
  Pierced the heart of a grizzly bear
  About to eat a child.

"When the posse caught up with Rattlesnake,
  Jake drawled with a sneer,
  'Sorry the sheriff got in the way.
  I was aimin' for that bear.'"

Jimmy jumped up. "That ain't so! The ding-danged liar. He was gunnin' for the sheriff all the time!" I pulled his shirt and he sat down again.

"The deputy laughed like he didn't believe—
Jake was as bad as Nero—
But the mother cried with tears in her eyes,
'Oh Jake, you is a hero!'

"So Jake went free to rob and kill
With glee and no remorse,
And he picked his teeth with his Bowie knife
As he rode out on his horse.

"So if you see around your camp
A man with his eye on your stake,
Lock up your gold, your wife, your dog—
It might be Rattlesnake Jake."

"Whoo!" said Jimmy Whiskers, slapping Amos on the back. "That story is taller than it is wide." He laughed and swung Prairie onto his shoulders, and they went to talk Mama into a piece or two of dried corn cake to hold them until breakfast. But I sat still as a stone wall. Dag diggety, what if Rattlesnake Jake was real? What if he was one of our boarders? I started to laugh at the very idea when I thought of Mr. Coogan picking his teeth and scowling at me. What if Rattlesnake Jake was real and he was our boarder Mr. Coogan?

"Listen," I said later to Butte, "I have long thought there is something curious about Mr. Coogan. He doesn't dig or wash for gold. He has no job, no store, no obvious prospects. He just walks around all day, poking and prying, and at night sits and stares at his paper. I think he's up to no good. I think he could be Rattlesnake Jake."

Butte was skeptical. Even I wasn't absolutely convinced until I realized that *if* the story were true and *if* Rattlesnake Jake were real and *if* he were an outlaw, then there was likely to be a reward for capturing him. And *if* Mr. Coogan were Rattlesnake Jake and *if* I helped capture him, then the reward would be mine! I took to watching Mr. Coogan closely, but he did nothing more evil than eat and sleep and battle his way through the rain to the privy out back.

When the rain eased a bit, he left the shelter of the boarding house and walked around the town. I followed along whenever I could get free. He carried his mysterious piece of paper folded up inside his hat and took it out now and then to read and chuckle over. Butte reckoned it was a map to a lost gold mine but I was convinced it was a copy of "The Ballad of Rattlesnake Jake."

"Mama," I said finally, "we've got to send someone to Marysville for the sheriff. I think maybe Mr. Coogan is Rattlesnake Jake."

"He is Percival Coogan and no outlaw."

"But Mama, he seems very suspicious. He doesn't dig or hunt or gamble or drink. He walks around in the

rain and mumbles to himself and doesn't talk to anybody. What is he doing here?"

"He pays his eighteen dollars and twenty cents a
week, that's what he does. Now don't pester the man."

"But Mama . . ."

"But Mama nothing. Where do you get these
notions? Go light a fire in the yard. We got to boil these
sheets before it starts to rain again."

I kept on following Mr. Coogan, real careful and
sneaky-like to make sure neither he nor anyone else saw
me. With all the rain, the diggings looked as if an army
of pigs had rooted through there, and I slipped and
squished in the mud. Everything looked so different,
and I had to stay so far behind, that several times I got
lost and bumped into Mr. Coogan making his way
back. I shivered all the way home.

I followed him down to the river and back again, up
onto the bluff and down again, into the woods and out
again. Peeking through tent flaps, I saw him eyeing the
gold dust in Mr. Scatter's money drawer, watching the
card players and their bags of dust, snorting as liquor
and money passed by him in the saloon, but gathered
no evidence of evil deeds.

"What's up, little sister?" asked the Gent. "You look
as worried as a duck in the desert."

"It's Mr. Coogan. Don't you think it's suspicious,
him being here all this time and doing nothing to make
or spend money?"

"Mighty strange, but no crime."

"What if he is Rattlesnake Jake and he waylays you on the way back to town and leaves you to die with a bullet in your head and takes off with your gold?"

"Now, little sister, the man hasn't done anything illegal. But keep watching. You may be a hero yet."

I didn't want to be a hero—just wanted the reward. I knew I wasn't hero material, but Butte just might be.

"Butte," I said early one morning, "if Mr. Coogan is indeed Rattlesnake Jake, we are in grave danger—me and Prairie and golden-haired Sierra and your beloved Mama . . ." I piled it on, and before he knew it, rain or no rain, he and Sweetheart were heading toward Rocky Bar for the deputy.

Mama asked at supper, "Where's Butte, girl?"

"Call me Lucy?"

Mama frowned and said nothing.

"He's helping French Pete tote some supplies to Rocky Bar. He'll be back tomorrow," I said, looking down at my lap. I was of the opinion that lying was a bad thing to do and cautioned Prairie and Sierra always to tell the truth. But these were desperate circumstances, and money for Massachusetts was on the line, so I lied but looked at my lap in preference to meeting Mama's eyes.

The ugly boarder who was probably Rattlesnake Jake gave me his fishy cold stare but said nothing.

By next morning the rain had become a storm with thunder and lightning and a mighty wind that put me in mind of *The Swiss Family Robinson*. Mr. Coogan put on his boots and his fur-lined coat with the beaver collar and went out anyway. I stayed behind to wait for the deputy, but neither the boarder nor Butte came back that day.

The storm passed, and Butte and the deputy rode into town the next morning. Mr. Coogan had not come back. He never did come back. Seemed like he just wandered off into the storm, leaving his gear behind. The deputy, Amos Frogge, Mr. Scatter, and the Gent went out searching for him, but the rain had erased his trail and they never saw hide nor hair of him. They figured he was lost in the storm and drowned or was eaten by a grizzly. I thought he had hightailed it out of town after finding out that Butte had gone for the law.

Butte got a scolding from Mama, but I got a licking. "Tie down that imagination of yours and quit telling stories before you get someone into real trouble." I figured I had already gotten someone into real trouble. Me. I had to eat supper standing up.

"Guess his running away proves," I said to the Gent, who had decided to stay and try his luck in Lucky Diggins, "that he really was Rattlesnake Jake."

"Could be, little sister, could be, but it don't always pay to go by appearances," said the Gent, winking at me as he picked his teeth with his Bowie knife.

To this day I can't say for sure that Rattlesnake Jake was Mr. Coogan. But he could have been. Or the Gent. Or anybody. Or nobody. And I'll never know. Things like this that aren't true or false, right or wrong, really irritate me.

CHAPTER EIGHT

SPRING 1850

In which Mama gets into a temper, Sweetheart gets lost, and I hear something I wish I hadn't

With the spring the miners came back more numerous than ever, as if they had obeyed the biblical command to be fruitful and multiply. The tent was exploding with boarders, and that meant plenty of extra work. One Sunday Mama boiled over. She kicked my book out into the mud, slapped Prairie for eating the last flapjack, and bellowed at the Gent, "Quit mooning at me with those cow eyes of yours and go do something useful!" Finally she took a deep breath and said, "I'm going plumb crazy boiling beans and washing sheets and beating batter for flapjacks. I've got to get out for a while, take a walk, see the mountain oaks putting out their green.

Prairie can mind Sierra and mend those stockings sitting on my chair. Butte, fetch us some greens from along the river for eating. Miss Lucy California, you give whoever shows up his dinner, fetch us a few loads of kindling, start boiling the potatoes, and I will be home in time to eat supper with you."

Sunday supper was the one meal when all the boarders and all the family and even miners who spent the week upriver in tents but had dust to spare would gather together, crowding around the rough plank table on benches, boxes, and the barrels that had held the meat and sauerkraut salted down for winter. Mama would set the table with bowls of potatoes, maybe a squirrel or rabbit stew, or beans with salt pork and molasses, some of her hard dry bread, and strong brown butter all the way from Boston. The miners were extra hungry after a whole day spent doing such despised chores as washing shirts, mending holes in their pants, and rubbing bear fat on their boots to keep the water out.

This Sunday I wrote a letter to Gram and Grampop— *We had biscuits and deer fat and boiled turnips for dinner, and I remembered Gram's oyster stew. I thought to write and ask you to mail me some and saw in my imagination Snowshoe Ballou coming up over the pass from French Creek with his letter bag dripping oyster stew and every skunk, badger, and weasel in the Sierra on his trail.* Butte took a bath—"What do you mean, dirt? I jist got dark feet." Asa Tooney pulled out an *Illustrated Police*

60

Gazette he got in Marysville—"Git yer mitts off'n that so's I kin read it. Gol durn it, you wrinkled it, you son of a gun. Watch out, now the cover's torn. Take that, you—" Dag diggety, I needed fresh air, too.

After a stop at the general store, where I traded gold dust for some of last year's licorice, hard as rock candy and twice as dusty, I lay luxuriating in the afternoon sunshine, skirt hiked up to my knees, making up stories about magic and miracles and singing "Amazing Grace," "Turkey in the Straw," and "Woodman, Spare That Tree." Tree! Dag diggety! I had forgotten the danged wood! Mama, already hopping mad, would likely skin me.

I bit my lip and tried to think. I didn't have time to make the three or four trips up the ravine necessary to fill the kindling box. Butte wasn't back yet. Prairie was watching Sierra. Well, then, I would take Sweetheart and some baskets. The work would go faster, and I'd be home in time to start the potatoes.

I got Sweetheart from her shed, threw the rope halter around her neck, and tied a basket on each side. Sweetheart switched her ears one at a time, first the brown one, then the white one, and let herself be dragged up the ravine path.

The path twisted and turned, reaching high enough so the air was cooler, the gnarled oaks dripped with mistletoe, and the meadows were blotched brown with mud and green with the promise of spring. I threw sticks and twigs and pinecones into the baskets, humming to myself as I pushed and pulled the mule along.

In a small clearing wild strawberries bloomed. I dropped Sweetheart's halter and, sitting cross-legged on the new grass, wove the leaves and flowers into wreaths, one for myself and one that I looped over Sweetheart's white ear. Sweetheart laughed or complained—I couldn't tell which, since she always sounded like a parlor organ out of tune—and then ate her wreath.

Through the brush I could see a small tower of interlaced branches and grass. I walked around it, looking carefully. A tower for a tiny Rapunzel, I decided, and spent a while imagining the prince climbing up Rapunzel's hair and the witch coming. But neither the prince nor the witch showed up, and I soon moved on.

Coming down a rise, I saw there to the left, as plain as day, a tree branching in a Y—what we called back home a wishing tree, for if you sat in it and wished, you would surely get your heart's desire. With a big smile I clambered up into the crotch, closed my eyes, and wished: *My heart's desire is to go home to Massachusetts.*

From my perch in the tree I looked around. The sun was low in the sky, and there were trees as far as I could see. Some were pink or white with blossoms, others were the soft green of new leaves, but most were the near-black evergreens that grew so densely up here. In the distance I could see a small clearing and a mule walking its stubborn slow mule's walk. . . . Sweetheart!

Was it Sweetheart? Where had I left her? Where was she now? And where was I?

I looked around again. There were the same pines as at Lucky Diggins, but no river. The same bramble bushes, but no creek. The same oaks, but no tents. I better go back, I thought. Trouble was, I didn't know where that was. The trees all looked alike, large leafy arms reaching for me and above all that huge bottomless bowl of a sky.

I jumped down and ran around awhile, getting more and more confused. From time to time I'd hear a gunshot and shout, "I'm here, Mama, over here," sure that Mama was back and worried about me and had set out with a searching party, which was signaling. "Here, Mama, here," I called as the sun got lower and the gunshots fainter and fainter.

Finally I flung myself down into the dust and cried. I am as good as dead, I thought. I'll starve or die of cold or be killed by a grizzly. All they will find are bones. And a bit of yellow hair, clinging to my skull.

"What you crying about?" asked Prairie.

Prairie! "What in Sam Hill are you doing here?" I asked, wiping my nose on my hand and my hand on my skirt.

"Mama thent me. You're late for thupper," Prairie said. Her front tooth had finally fallen out.

"How did you find me?"

"Took the path up the ravine, turned left a thpell, and there you wath. Let'th go."

"We can't go. We're lost."

"Luthy," Prairie said, "you are the thilliest girl. We're barely two treeth and a hill from home."

I explained about being lost and wandering and losing Sweetheart. We looked around for the mule awhile, calling her name and trying to make mule noises, but got no response. So I followed my little sister back to Lucky Diggins, head hanging but heart glad I wasn't lost or worse. Mama will be happy to see I'm not dead, I thought.

"Here we are, Mama," said Prairie. "She wath jutht out back a wayth."

Mama turned to me. She didn't look happy. "You forgot to start the potatoes."

I said nothing about the mule while we ate our cabbage soup and salt pork stewed with turnips and Butte's wild greens and cowslip pickle and a batter pudding, but no potatoes.

After supper, after the dishes were washed and the pots scoured with sand and the dirt floor swept with a corn-husk broom, the Gent pulled out his fiddle and the newest boarder, Rusty Hawkins, his mouth harp, and we had music. I had a talk with Mama and then sat down to write a letter by the light of a lard-oil lamp.

Dear Gram and Grampop,

Sometimes I wonder whether your daughter ever was a child herself. The Bible says we should strive for perfection, not be perfect all the time. I know it was my fault that Sweetheart is lost—a long story I will tell another time—and our extra income with her, but I think taking my money is beyond justice.

After supper, I told Mama about losing the mule. I expected she would holler and maybe even cuss, she's so Californiaized, but instead she said calmly, "Sixteen dollars."

"For what?" I enquired.

"For the cost of the mule."

"Where am I to get sixteen dollars?"

"From that smelly old crock you're hoarding dust and money in."

I told her that was my going-home-to-Massachusetts money, and she just sniffed and said, "Well, you'll likely never get there if you keep on doing bob-stupid things like losing our mule. Sixteen dollars."

So my pickle crock is a blame sight lighter tonight and I have been sent in disgrace to my bed, and I am angry as a horned toad on a fry pan, as Jimmy would say. How did nice people like you ever get such a daughter?

I put this letter under my straw mattress until I could decide whether to send it. I could hear the sounds of music and laughter, and although I was not about to give Mama the satisfaction of seeing me watching, I peered around the blanket curtain.

They were dancing. The men who weren't dancing

with Mama or Prairie danced with each other, arguing over who would lead and who was stepping on whose feet. I loved to dance, all by myself in the meadow outside the house in Massachusetts on a warm summer night, but clunking around the boarding tent in the arms of a miner in need of a bath was not my idea of dancing.

Soon the Gent put down his fiddle and swung Mama around to the music of Rusty's mouth harp. She laughed and looked very young, like she forgot for a minute about lost income and lost mules. If I hadn't been so dag diggety angry, I might even have felt bad about adding to her troubles.

Finally, when everybody was danced out, they rested their blisters a spell while Mama boiled molasses down for taffy. Greasing up their hands with lard, the boarders took turns pulling the candy into long strands and doubling it and pulling it again until it was a consistency to eat. By that time it seemed there was more of the gray, sticky candy on their hands and mouths and shirt fronts than in the pan. Some of the miners commenced playing dominoes while others drifted off to bed or to the saloon to drink too much and sleep in a drunken huddle on the saloon floor until morning.

I heard the Gent say: "I sure do fancy that woman."

Who? I thought, moving closer and picking up mugs and plates, the better to listen.

"Who don't?" said Rusty.

"Yeah. Well, I aim to marry her."

Who? I thought again. Belle Scatter? Milly from the saloon?

"You polecat, what makes you think she'd have you?"

The Gent said, with a smile in his voice, "My charm, my good looks, and my money."

Rusty slapped him hard on the back. "If that ain't the beatingest thing I ever heard. Why, you got the charm of a mosquito, the good looks of a hog's butt, and less money than a greenhorn in a gambling house. I think she'd do better to take Jimmy."

"Nevertheless," said the Gent, "I aim to marry Arvella."

I dropped the stack of plates, and the rattling of tin rumbled like thunder through the tent. Mama? They were talking about Mama? The Gent wanted to marry *Mama*? As if Pa were just worms' meat and not Pa anymore, now he was dead!

Mama was all I had left, and I sure didn't want to give her away to some man, even one with curly hair and a fiddle, like the Gent. My heart beat like rain on a canvas roof as I went looking for Mama.

Mama wasn't in the front tent or in the big tent the boarders slept in. Thinking maybe she'd gone to the necessary out back, I took a candle and stepped into the night. A moving wisp of mist uncovered the face of the moon, and for a minute I was transported back to

67

Massachusetts, where Pa was whispering, "California, get up. Come and look. Come," and there right outside the door, under a midwinter moon, a group of cotton-tails, freed by the clear weather from their underground burrows, were frolicking on the crusted snow.

Then the mountain mist covered the moon again. Pa was gone, and I was back in Lucky Diggins, looking for Mama.

Mama stood near the stump all alone.

"What are you doing, Mama? There's no stars or anything to look at."

I could see her smile in the light from the tent flap. "I'm just talking to your pa."

I felt easier. The Gent would have a long row to hoe if he wanted Mama.

CHAPTER NINE

SPRING / SUMMER 1850
In which Butte and I both get educated

The warm days of spring brought an explosion of wildflowers—mustard, lupine, and golden poppies, wild lilac and wood anemone—that nearly concealed the holes, pits, and ditches the miners left behind. Spring also meant we could finally remove the heavy winter underwear that covered us neck to ankles in scratchy gray wool. I felt almost bare naked and so free.

We finally moved into the wooden boarding house. Though it was little and crude by Buttonfields standards, the feel of a real house above my head and under my feet just about made up for the added chore of scrubbing the floor with clean river sand and the hog-bristle brush. There was room for twice as many beds,

69

which meant twice as many biscuits, twice as many beans, and twice as many sheets to boil in great kettles outside, pound with battling sticks, and spread on bushes to dry.

As if all this weren't enough, Mama decided that Butte was getting too rough and wild and uneducated and that I should teach him after supper each day and some on Sunday afternoon.

"What do you mean, uneducated?" said Butte when I told him. "I already know forty-eight words for liquor."

"You lie. You don't," I said.

"Do."

"Don't."

Butte stood up and cleared his throat like someone about to make a speech. "Hooch, cactus juice, catgut, cougar's milk, gator sweat, jack-a-dandy, kingdom come, knock-me-down, mother's milk, throat tickler, firewater, alky, gullet wash, tangle legs, diddle, courage, bug juice, corpse reviver, popskull, stingo, blue ruin, panther piss, pig sweat, rotgut, sheep wash, snake juice, whoopie water, witches' piss, lightning flash, neck oil, ammunition, oil of joy, joy water, tiger milk, nose paint, sorrow drowner, bosom friend, snake medicine, bust head, cut throat, coffin varnish, craw rot, liquid fire, smile, blackstrap, corn juice, gut warmer, and chain lightning. Two more and I'll have fifty. Reckon that will be some sort of record."

I was impressed in spite of myself.

"And I know ten words for saloon: rumhole, mughouse, groggery . . ."

"Butte."

"And seven words for privy: outhouse, ajax, necessary, shi—"

"Butte!" This was Mama. That settled it. Butte had to quit sweeping the saloon and get educated.

Dear Miss Homer,

I bring you greetings from Mama and all of us at Lucky Diggins. Thank you for the box of books. When it came, I just sat and stared at the miracle of a parcel with my name on it. I thought I'd make a plan for opening it over a long period of time, so I could savor it. Open the box one day, remove the contents another. Instead, I was so excited, I just ripped the box open and sat down on the floor with the packing paper piled around me and my chores undone.

I took each book, smelled the paper and glue, felt its weight in my hand, and rubbed the raised letters on the cover and spine. I have lined them up on my shelf in the order in which I will read them. I am reading The Corsican Brothers *now and think to start next either* Evelina *or* The Book of British Ballads. *I plan on saving* The History of Little Goody Two-Shoes *for last, thank you nonetheless for sending it. The packing paper I have saved for writing letters.*

The books got here at just the right time. I am to educate

Butte, and I would get mighty tired of hearing him butcher Ivanhoe.

Please send my greetings to the class, especially Essie Beck and Opal McCurdy. Tell them not to forget me before I figure a way to get back. I have been planning to write them but I fear that they never could understand my life here. How could I tell them about living with a bunch of men who never wash or change their clothes or speak below a bellow, in a space so small I can lie in bed and stir the beans on the stove without getting up? Those of us lucky enough to have a house instead of a tent paste calico and packing paper on the wall to keep the wind and dirt and bugs out. No one has a book or a new dress or flowers growing outside the door.

Besides, postage costs so danged much.

Summer came and was very hot and—impossible as it seemed after that wet winter—very dry. Where had all the water gone? No one washed body or sheets or shirts. Mama boiled potatoes in such a little bit of water that they scorched and Jimmy took to calling them "smoked potatoes."

Prairie had planted beans and carrots and potatoes, hoping to store enough to see us through another wet winter if necessary, but the plants grew limp and sorry-looking in the heat. In August, when the river dried up, we looked to lose them all. So Butte and I took to walking downriver to the Forks, filling buckets in the Yuba, which still ran, warm and shallow but wet, and lugging them back to Lucky Diggins.

I thought to use the walking time to continue Butte's education. "If we walk six miles each way, that is two times six, which is how many miles?"

"Too many."

"Be serious, Butte."

"I'm mighty serious. This ain't no fun and you're making it worse with this two times two stuff. I'm tired enough and I'm certainly hot enough and I think I'm educated enough, too. Why do I have to know two times everything?"

"Butte, even miners got to know how to subtract and multiply to figure out, oh, their expenses and whether Mr. Scatter or some banker is cheating them."

"I don't aim to be a miner."

"You don't? I thought you had gold fever and wanted to do nothing but search for color and strike it rich."

"Not hardly. Too much dirt. I want to be the captain of a ship, a beautiful sailing ship that goes to the South Seas and the Sandwich Islands and maybe even around the world. I was never so happy as on that ship from Boston to San Francisco."

The very memory set my stomach to churning, so I changed the subject back to arithmetic. For a while we practiced adding big numbers in our heads—4,786 plus 392—but we concentrated so hard on carrying numbers that we forgot we were carrying buckets and sloshed nearly half our hard-gotten water over our boots. We moved on to history.

"Sea captains don't need to know history," said Butte.

"Of course they do."

"This one don't."

"Butte, you don't even know what history is."

"Do so. It's old stuff that nobody cares about any-more."

"Did you ever stop to think that someday we will be history, part of the great Gold Search or some such? Maybe we'll be in history books—the mighty Whipples of Whippletown who struck it rich in California."

"No more educating today, Lucy. Tell me more about the mighty Whipples."

"Well," I said, relieved to be imagining instead of educating, "there is Mrs. Whipple, the mother, who serves tea every afternoon in her big mansion and wears ruby velvet dresses and a big hat with a bird's nest on it. And the oldest daughter, Lucy, who is very beautiful and sought after by all the men but who prefers to lie in a hammock on her green and glorious Massachusetts estate and read. She does not eat oatmeal or possum or boiled milk and bread, and never has to chop onions or lug water in lard buckets. Next is Captain Butte, the famous mariner."

"What's a mariner?"

"A sailor. I told you you don't know everything. He sails the Pacific Ocean from San Francisco to the

Sandwich Islands and has a beautiful Kanaka wife who waits with flowers and pineapples for his return. Next there would have been Ocean Whipple, but she died. Then Prairie . . ."

"Say more about Ocean. Nobody talks about her, as though she never was. I remember Golden and the pneumonia, but all I know about Ocean is she was there and then not there."

We stopped to rest our arms and take a few bites of the cold potatoes I carried in my apron pocket. "Papa used to talk to me about her, but Mama won't," I told Butte. "Never said her name to me as far as I can recall. Papa used to say she was no bigger than a minute, with yellow ringlets and a dimple in her chin. She called him Popsy.

"Once Mama took her through the woods to Oakbridge. You and I were just getting over the quinsy and stayed with Gram, and Prairie and Sierra weren't born yet. On the way back from town, Mama sat down to get a stone out of her shoe and Ocean disappeared. They searched a mighty long time, but nobody ever saw her again. We don't know was it Indians or outlaws or wolves or what." I shivered. It seemed a whole lot more scary to me out here than it had back home, like something that could happen to anyone, not just a toddling baby.

"Do you think she's dead?"

"I reckon so. No one rightly knows."

"If she's alive, I wonder what she looks like now." Butte snickered. "If she's dead, I wonder what she looks like."

"Butte, how morbid and awful."

"I wonder what Pa looks like now."

"Butte!"

I hurried on ahead, bucket bumping against my legs and more of the precious water splashing my skirt. But Butte, skinny and fast like Pa, caught up with me. "I don't mean to be morbid, Luce. He's still my pa, even now, and I wonder what he looks like, is all. Is his skin hanging in tatters? Is he just bones? Are his fingers and toes—"

"Butte, you're making me sick. Why do you think about things like that?"

"Sometimes I like to think of things that are bad or scary, kind of like practicing for being brave. I have to be brave now that Pa's dead and except for me you're all females."

"Females can be brave too, Butte."

"Yeah, but you ain't very and I'm the next oldest so I reckon it's up to me. I don't think I'd be near as brave if I didn't feel I had to."

I stopped in surprise. I never knew that. Figured Butte was just naturally all guts and go-get-it.

I put down the bucket and rumpled his hair. It shone red in the sun. Like Pa's. "Seems like I'm getting educated today as well as you."

Dear Gram and Grampop,

All of a sudden I am grown mighty popular and it is all due to the box of books from Miss Homer. Men I have never spoken to this past whole year come up to me, hat in hand, and say, "Excuse me entirely, little sister, but I hear you might have some books for borrying."

I have become a one-person lending library. My library has two rules:

1. I get to read books first.

2. No chewing tobacco stains.

I used to have a third rule—Return what you borrow to ME. Do not lend it to someone else—but everyone broke that rule. Besides, the books always come back to me eventually, so I have eliminated rule number three.

Some of my books have gone fifty miles or so up and down the river and have come back with notes inside: "Ripping good story, miss!" or "What a conbobberation about nothing" or "Might you have one where the heroine has yellow hair and is called Marthy?"

One miner wrapped about five dollars' worth of dust in a cigarette paper and put it between pages twenty-four and twenty-five of "Rip Van Winkle" and it was still there when the book came back to me. I have used it toward paying off Bean Belly Thompson for carrying the books.

Next time you visit Pa's grave, please plant some flowers on it for Butte and me, larkspur if you can find it for we have that here and I would like to think we are looking at the same thing, even if I look at the flowers and he the roots. Mama says Pa is in Heaven with God, but the last time I saw him he was in a box in the ground in Massachusetts, so that is how I tend to think of him. Not that I don't believe in God. I do. I'm just not sure that I believe in Heaven, at least not like I believe in the public library.

Writing about Pa made me more than ever homesick for Massachusetts, so I got my pickle crock and tried to guess how much money was left in it. I counted the coins and attempted to weigh the gold dust by holding it in one hand and a half pound of lard in the other. I still didn't know just how much was there, but I knew it was not near enough. Sighing a big sigh, I went to the kitchen to chop onions and cabbage for slaw.

CHAPTER TEN

AUTUMN 1850

In which I, though unwilling, pick berries in the wilderness and am rewarded with a new friend

September came clear and hot. Blackberry weather. And dewberry, elderberry, and huckleberry.

"Why do I have to go picking and not Prairie?" I asked Mama. "She wants to go and I don't."

"Prairie is only seven. I don't want her wandering alone out there."

"Mama, you shouldn't want *me* wandering alone. I'm the one who gets lost and Prairie's the one who finds me. She'll do better than I will."

"Nevertheless," Mama said, and I knew that I and not Prairie would be berry picking.

Each morning I gathered up my wits and my

buckets, hid *The Count of Monte Cristo* under my apron, and trudged away to the hillside off Ranger Creek. The hot summer had dried the grass and turned the oats yellow too soon, but the berry bushes still tangled along the creek.

I quickly settled into the work. From late morning to noon I'd read in the shade of a tree. At noon I'd eat my biscuits and cold gravy. Early afternoon, yearning for the cool waters of spring, I'd stick my feet in the warm, sticky mud of the creek and read some more. Late afternoon would find me running from bush to bush, grabbing frantically at whatever berries I could reach. And at night I'd try and explain to Mama why berry picking was going so slow.

After several days of this I reached an especially exciting part of the book, and before I knew it, late afternoon was almost gone and the first evening stars were getting ready to come out. I jumped up and ran for the buckets.

They were full.

From a bush came a voice, slow and soft: "Don't be scared, missy. I noted that you looked to be running out of daylight afore you run out of book, so I thought to lend a hand."

"Thank you," I whispered, and took off for home, buckets bouncing and spilling berries all the way, wondering was it elves or fairies or was God speaking to me from a bush the way He spoke to Moses.

The next day I looked around a little for tiny footprints or signs of burning before I sat down to read.

"Morning, missy," said the voice from the bush. "Looks like we're in the same business, you hunting God's bounty in the bushes and me in the creeks."

The stranger parted the bushes and looked through. He was no elf or fairy. He was a grown man with curly hair and whiskers. And he was brown. Very brown. Not like the sailors from the Sandwich Islands we had seen in San Francisco. Browner. He was not an Indian, for he wore more clothes than the Indians I'd seen around Lucky Diggins. Nor was he from South America like Friday in *Robinson Crusoe,* for his hair was not long and straight like Friday's.

I had never met a brown man before. There were none in our small Massachusetts town. I had heard that the barber in Acorn was the kind of brown man called colored man. Was this a colored man like the barber? My thoughts were so busy I stood stock-still and stared.

The brown man came out from behind the bush, lifted his pan in a salute, and walked down to the creek, where he swished that pan in the muddy ooze all day trying to wash gold from the gravel. I picked some and then ran home to help Mama make soap.

"Mama," I said, carrying out a bucket of meat scraps and bacon grease, "I saw a brown man. A colored man."

Mama looked up from the bubbling tub but said nothing. I could barely see her for the smoke from the fire and the steam rising from the kettle.

"Why are some people brown?" I asked her.

"Some people are brown like some people got red hair. We all belong to God," Mama said, stirring the boiling fat and ashes in the kettle.

"Are colored people same as us?"

"Probably have harder lives but otherwise I reckon so, though not everybody agrees. Some people think what you look like makes you what you are." Mama straightened up and stretched. "Only have to know Jimmy Whiskers to know that ain't so, such a good gentle heart in such an ugly bear of a man."

I saw the brown man every day as I continued picking berries and soon came to trust his soft voice, sad eyes, and kind face behind the scruffy beard. Sometimes he spoke, sometimes not. Sometimes he left me berries or greens, pigweed or miner's lettuce, which I took home for supper.

His name was Joe. He sang while he worked, songs full of sadness and longing.

"What you readin' there, missy?" he asked once.

"A tale of romance and adventure," I said.

Well, nothing would do then but for him to join me. Soon we were both sitting with our feet in the mud of Ranger Creek, swapping stories. He told me of Anansi the Spider, old John and the Devil, and Bruh Rabbit, who was puny but smart. Then I would read out loud a spell. He greatly admired my reading and asked all the right questions: "Lord, what made him do that?" and "Couldn't she tell what a villain he was?"

Sometimes we shared my noon dinner, but he'd never eat bacon or salt beef. "Give me hog and hominy, and I'll live on hominy," he said. "Pigs is living critters treated like things, the way I was, and I'll not be eatin' 'em."

I finally got up the courage to ask the question Mama had failed to answer satisfactorily. "Why are some people brown, Joe?"

"Good Lord saw fit, and I figure I don't need a better reason than that."

Seemed like that was all the answer I was going to get. "How did you come here? No other people like you around."

Joe wiped the sweat off his face with his sleeve. "I spent all my born days on Mr. Sawyer's place in Virginia, jist Sawyer and the missus and me and four other slaves. I never can remember anyone of my own. Mr. Sawyer, he decides that farm ain't enough for him, and he brung us out west. Near the Big Muddy, Mrs. Sawyer says, 'John, I ain't going a step farther' and set fire to the wagon." Joe scooped up a mess of muddy water in his pan. "Lord, what a stubborn lady. They hadn't settled the dispute when she up and died of camp fever." He whirled the pan so that the water and lighter particles splashed out. "So Mr. Sawyer bought another wagon and we come to Paddy's Bar, miners like thousands of others. At least we five were. Since Mrs. Sawyer died, Mr. Sawyer took to drink and jist sat and waved his rifle about and beat us if he thought there wasn't enough dust at the end of the day." Joe picked through the muck left at the bottom of the pan, looking for bits of color. Nothing in that pan. He stooped and scooped up another.

"One day a scraggly old fella on a mule says, 'Why do you take it? No slavery in California, you know.' I didn't know if he was right or he was wrong, but I saw this as my chance to take off, saying to Mr. Sawyer, 'You can shoot me, but you can't own me no more.' Mr. Sawyer, he was too dumb and too drunk to know was this true or not, just fell off his horse, so I left. Took nothing but this here pan and a pick and a bedroll; figured he owed me for all my free labor."

Joe stood up straight and stretched, then stooped down to scoop again. "I ain't found much since, just work tired-out claims others have abandoned. But what I find is mine. The belly that gets hungry is mine and the shoulders that ache are mine and the hands that bleed are mine and no other man's. I ain't no slave out here. While I'm on my own, I'm as good as free, and being free is everything."

His story sounded to me like one of Amos Frogge's ballads—coming across the country by wagon, escaping from a drunken master, fleeing alone into the wilderness to search for gold, living as a runaway slave.

One thing I didn't understand. "What's it mean being a slave?" I knew about slaves in ancient Rome, but somehow I didn't think Mr. Sawyer planned to feed Joe to the lions.

"A slave is a fella who belongs body and soul to another fella and has to do what he is told and go where he is bid and gets beat if he don't do it fast enough or good enough."

"Like being a child," I said.

"Nowhere near, missy. Chil'ren is loved and taken care of. A slave don't even own his own life or his wife or babies. A slave is a thing, like an axe or a bucket. Can be bought or sold or killed, whatever his owner wants. Ain't no light thing for a man to be a slave." He threw his pan high into the air and caught it with a grunt. "And I ain't one, not out here."

As the nights began to grow cold, I worried for Joe, sleeping in his bedroll on the shores of Ranger Creek and living on nuts and wild greens.

"Mama, with winter coming, we're going to have some empty beds, aren't we?"

"I reckon, but not too many, I hope," said Mama, who was chopping potatoes and onions for rabbit hash.

"Couldn't we rent one to my friend Joe? I know he could pay. He's had some luck washing for color."

"Who's Joe?"

"The brown man I told you about, at Ranger Creek."

Mama stopped chopping for a minute.

"Lucy," she said, "I can't rent a bed to a colored man. All my other boarders would leave."

"Not Jimmy."

Mama commenced chopping vigorously, as if she had to make up for that minute of rest. "Probably not Jimmy, but everyone else."

"Why?"

"Because lots of people think colored folk aren't fit to live with white people."

"Why not?"

"I don't exactly know why not. Scared maybe. Anyway, Mr. Scatter would never allow it."

"But, Mama, what will happen when it rains and snows and the ice—"

"Lord, Lucy, don't pester me. Your friend can sleep in Sweetheart's old shed and I'll make him breakfast and supper for ten dollars a week if he'll eat it outside. That's all I can do."

I ran back to Ranger Creek and told Joe.

"Now that's mighty nice, young lady, but I'll be fine—"

"No, you won't be fine when it rains ice for days at a time and you have no food and no fire and no shelter. Be reasonable, Joe."

"I suppose I could manage ten dollars a week if I traded some of this dust and maybe got me a town job. But . . ."

"But what, Joe? Spit it out." I sounded to my own ears like Mama.

"Out here where I see no one but you, I am a free man. But I worry that Mr. Sawyer or some other white man will find me and take me off to be a slave again. A town, even a little town, is too dangerous for me. I best stay out here."

"You have to come. You've never seen winters like we got here, with ice storms and buckets of rain." Besides, I liked having him around. We were friends. I enjoyed his stories, and he admired my reading. Not many people admired anything I did. "Please, Joe."

Joe was silent. Then he sighed. "Well then, Miss Lucy, now I got me this fine place to live, all I need is a name."

I stopped my gleeful hopping and spinning to ask, "Isn't Joe your name?"

"Mr. Sawyer, he called all the men Joe so's he didn't have to bother remembering who was who. I think I need me a real name that belongs only to me."

I thought of *The Count of Monte Cristo* under my pillow. "Maximilian," I said. "Maximilian is such an elegant name."

Joe rubbed his chin. "Maximilian don't seem to suit me, missy."

"Ivanhoe or Damian or Appassionato?"

"No, seems like I don't feel like an Appassionato, thanks all the same."

A few days later, when Joe showed up to claim his bed in the shed, I said, "I have a present for you."

"You ain't got no call to get me presents, missy."

"Nevertheless, here it is." I stretched out my fist and slowly opened it. The hand was empty.

Joe looked at me.

"It's a name. For you. My father's name. Bernard."

"Bernard." Joe rubbed his beard. "Bernard. It's a mighty fine name, missy. A name I'd be proud to carry. Bernard."

"There's more," I added, sticking out my other fist. "A last name."

He blinked.

I opened my hand. "Freeman," I said.

CHAPTER ELEVEN

SPRING 1851

*In which a wandering preacher saves Butte's body
and Amos Frogge's soul, and my new
Massachusetts scheme goes awry*

Clyde Claymore came riding into Lucky Diggins
with the wildflowers the next spring. He was a big man,
tall and bulky, dressed in rusty black linsey-woolsey
and a wide-brimmed black hat. He rode into town on a
mule so small that Clyde's enormous square-toed boots
dragged in the mud. I thought Clyde could more easily
carry that mule than the mule carry Clyde.

I first saw him from the boarding house porch, where
the broom and I were engaged in our constant war
against mud.

"Young lady," he boomed as though calling in a
canyon, "where is the town of Lucky Diggins?"

"This is it," I said.

"The rest of it, I mean."

"This is all."

"All? This little place?"

Surprised, I looked around. California was now one of the great United States of America, and Lucky Diggins was booming. The town boasted Mr. Scatter's saloon and a new drinking place opened by a gambler called Poker John Lewis, a general store of wood as well as the boarding house with a real porch, the smithy, the card parlor, a supply store with picks and axeheads and shovels, a restaurant that served flapjacks, beans, and bacon, and ten or so cabins and tents in town and maybe fifty more stretched up and down the river. And on Friday, Saturday, and Sunday nights when miners came down from the hills, the population swelled by hundreds and there weren't nearly enough places for them all to eat and drink and sleep.

Now I saw Lucky Diggins again through the eyes of a stranger. Small and dirty, the town smelled of privies. The streets were mud and dust, littered with oyster tins, ham bones, and broken shovels. Nearby trees had been butchered to stumps in order to erect the ugly raw wood buildings rising along the street. Worst of all, it wasn't Massachusetts and never would be.

I turned my back on the stranger and went into the kitchen to stir the supper beans. My pickle crock, I thought. It had been sitting there untouched for months. There was no way to earn money in the winter unless I could sell mud to someone, but now that spring was here, I determined to get out the crock, dust it off, and start working my way back home once more. Time to fire up the pie business again.

I sighed. More getting up early, traipsing up and down the river, and trying to avoid crazy men in their union suits.

The big man came into the kitchen. "Young lady," he boomed.

"Ma!"

"Don't shout, Lucy. I'm here. Want a bed, mister?" she asked, wiping her hands on her apron and giving a cold, appraising eye to the stranger and the mud on his boots.

"I do indeed, ma'am, praise the Lord. I am Brother Clyde Claymore, minister of the Free and Independent Church of Christ's Brethren, come to save souls, and I wonder if there is about here a family that might like the pleasure of taking me in for a spell in Jesus' name."

Mama frowned. Our pastor in Massachusetts had baptized and married and buried Whipples for forty years and had eaten Sunday suppers and Tuesday lunches with them and had his socks darned and his coat pressed by one Whipple woman or another. But he had refused to bury Pa because Pa was not a church-going man, and ever since, Mama said she had no use for religious men. Said they left a bad taste in her mouth, like old mushrooms.

Finally she answered him. "There ain't many families around here at all. There are the Flaggs, but you won't like staying there unless you like sleeping with coyotes, them being the wild sort. Mr. Scatter might do, but he has an unmarried daughter with marriage in mind, and most of the rest live in shacks or tents and don't have room to swing a cat by the tail, much less take in a stranger. This is about the only place in town to stay."

"Then I will stay here, ma'am, thank you very much."   .

"Mr. Scatter gets eighteen dollars and twenty cents for each of these beds each week and I'm not about to give one away. You got eighteen twenty, Mr. Claymore?"

"Brother Claymore, ma'am," he rejoined, doffing his hat and flourishing it before him as if he were going to sweep the floor. "And you are Sister . . . ?"

"Sister nobody, Mr. Claymore. I am Mrs. Whipple and I have little affection for men of the cloth. Come back with eighteen twenty and you may have a bed. Good day to you. And next time wipe your feet."

Seemed like Brother Clyde Claymore didn't have $18.20, for he got back on his tiny mule and rode into the camps up along the river, looking for shelter and praising God. The walls of the ravine rang with his call for all to forsake their wicked ways and accept God, hallelujah, and by the way perhaps make a small offering so Brother Claymore could get some food and a bed, amen.

For all he was so big, Brother Claymore was gentle and soft-looking, an easy butt for the jokes of the miners. For a while he and his doings provided most of our supper conversation.

"That crazy Clyde," said Amos one night. "Know what he did today? Leo Mack told him that Flapjack was yearnin' and yowlin' and missin' his wife and kiddies something fierce. Flapjack, who has no wife and no family and never said a kind word to nobody in all his years! So Clyde went and hugged Flapjack right there at Flat Camp in front of the whole crew. Thought old Flapjack would bust a gut."

Jimmy slapped his knee and shouted, "That ain't nothin'. In a voice loud enough to wake snakes, he told Leo Mack he loved him! We was hootin' and whistlin', but ole Clyde stood there grinnin' like a possum eatin' a yellow jacket. Said nothing we could do or say would stop him from loving Leo. Gol durn, pardon me, ma'am, if Crazy wasn't so durned big, Leo would have pitched him in the water."

The Gent said Brother Clyde wanted nothing more than to preach to the miners, but they hid when they heard him coming, so he'd just stand there and preach to the trees. "I said to him, 'Clyde,' I said, 'you'd do a blame sight better if you worked that hard at mining,' but he just laughed and said he *was* mining, mining for souls."

As I peddled my pies—mock apple made of crackers and a bit of cider vinegar until summer brought real fruit—I bumped into Clyde now and again, riding that tiny mule. Clyde called the mule Apostle because the mule, like the Apostles, was wise as a serpent and harmless as a dove.

Somehow Clyde was picking up pinches of gold dust here and there, and after a week or so those pinches amounted to a bit. He came back, dumped it into Mama's lap, and said, "Might this be eighteen dollars and twenty cents, ma'am? I'm mighty tired of sleeping with my mule."

"Looks to be, Brother Claymore," said Mama, softening a little toward a boarder with gold. "I will get it weighed at the store. Go wipe your boots." Although Mr. Scatter had been accused from time to time of dampening his hands when weighing gold so some of the dust would stick to his fingers, he had the only scales in town. Gold was sixteen dollars an ounce, or about a dollar a pinch, but the scales were the only way to be sure.

So we were joined at suppers by Brother Clyde. One night the Gent asked him what kind of church he was minister of.

"Well now," he replied, "that's an interesting story. The Lord called me to serve Him, thank you, Lord, but He didn't tell me how. So I just started out preaching the benefits of prunes and proverbs until someone asked me that very same question, what kind of church was I a minister of. 'Well sir,' I replied, 'that I can't rightly say, but I know what kind of minister I am. I am a minister who has little taste for sects and isms, for being on my knees, for preaching indoors to those who already believe and behave. I believe in love, turning the other cheek, Heaven and Hell, the power of God, and being a brother to all of like belief.' So I became founder of the Free and Independent Church of Christ's Brethren, and its bishop and only minister."

"You ever preach to wild Indians or get chased by pirates or redcoats?" Butte asked, his mouth full of potato. Everyone laughed. Seemed like my educating wasn't doing Butte too much good.

"No, I can't say so, young fella, though I been treed by grizzlies and run out of town by unbelievers, and I been beset by boils, rashes, ulcers, and the rheumatics. But as long as I was doing God's work, all was well."

He looked sad for a minute and then continued, in a voice much softer than his usual boom, "Now I'm thinking about packing up and moving on. Back to New Hampshire. There are always groups who need toting back east, so I'd get my way paid." Suddenly I was very interested.

Brother Clyde went on. "Don't know what else to do. I can't say I've done very well as a preacher. No converts, no followers. I thought to be having a prayer meeting by this time, but not a body around here will come. The good Lord doesn't need a spiritual father with no children, a shepherd without sheep, who labors long in the vineyards but grows no grapes."

The boarders all looked down at their plates. Feeling sorry for the man was one thing, but getting religion for his sake was more than they planned on. I, however, had a masterpiece of an idea. *If* Brother Clyde were to lead a group back east, and *if* Mama were to approve of him, then she might let me go with him!

The next day I started my campaign. "I somewhat like Brother Clyde, don't you, Mama?"

Mama poured potato water and yeast and flour into a big bowl and commenced mixing it with her hands. "You know how I feel about so-called men of God. I'm sure your pa up in Heaven is sitting closer to God than all the smug, strutting, hypocritical preachers in history." The dough got turned out onto the tabletop and kneaded harder than necessary.

"I don't think Brother Claymore is like that," I said.

"No matter. Sounds like he'll be gone soon anyway."

I decided to approach from the other side. "Brother Claymore," I asked one night, "what kind of religion do you preach? I mean, are there rules?"

"Well, Miss Lucy, I'm not much for rules. I preach free will and free grace and every man's salvation is between him and the Lord."

"What exactly does that mean? Do you believe people go to Hell?"

"Lucy!" warned Mama.

"That's all right, Sister Whipple. That's how young folk learn, asking questions."

"Mrs. Whipple," Mama muttered.

"Free will, Miss Lucy," Brother Claymore went on, "means people choose Heaven or Hell, God or the Devil, but I can't rightly tell who is going where and neither can anyone else, so I minister unto them all and refuse nothing."

"Would you ever refuse to bury someone because he was, well, a sinner, or greedy, or maybe not a church-going man?"

Mama scowled at me, but Brother Clyde answered. "No, can't say I would, Miss Lucy. The way I see it, we're all sinners time to time, and it does no good for me to shut up my bowels of compassion. My job is to help people find their way to God, and I can't see how not burying a man would help him or me or God any." He looked at Mama. "Finding God is what it's all about. Perhaps I could help you, Sister Whipple, find your way to God."

"Mrs. Whipple," said Mama, "and I know where and how to find God. It's just you men who claim to speak for Him I have trouble with."

"We ministers don't speak for God, Mrs. Whipple. God speaks through us. Trouble is sometimes we have a hard time figuring out what is God's voice and what Brother Claymore's."

Mama sniffed and Brother Claymore continued, "It is my opinion, after years of reading and studying and praying on the matter, that wicked churchgoers who do evil to their fellow men are cast out of God's sight, but good men are in Heaven with the Lamb of God, amen, whether they set foot in a church or not."

At that Mama smiled, and I felt like I was halfway packed and on my way back to Massachusetts!

The sun shone for a few days, and the melted snow running off the mountains swelled the rivers and creeks to dangerous levels. The miners had to be extra careful as they waded in and out, digging and washing the gravel, and even so a pan or a boot or a hat occasionally would come bobbing on the river right through town and out toward the sea.

One drizzly Tuesday morning, Butte slipped and fell into the river. He hit his head on a rock and, caught in the swift current, was swept downstream, miners running along the bank all the way, shouting and calling his name.

He stuck on some rocks at the bend close to town, and some miners nearby, busy trying not to listen to Brother Claymore, raced down to the banks, where they stood around deciding how to get Butte out without getting any of them in. They commenced pushing and shoving and arguing and were about to start spitting and punching when suddenly Butte broke free and began again his tumbling down the river.

Brother Clyde ran down, pulled off his coat and hat, and, "quicker than you can spit and holler howdy," Jimmy Whiskers said later, plunged into the river and tumbled and rumbled right after Butte. They banged into some rocks together, and finally Brother Clyde, with Butte tucked under his arm, rose from the water like a river god in a Greek myth.

A parade of wet miners followed Brother Claymore back to town, Butte draped over the tiny mule's back. If Mama were the type of woman to faint, that would have been the moment, I thought later, with Butte's limp body hanging sideways over Apostle and all those miners deserting the river on a Tuesday to accompany him back to town. But she didn't faint, didn't scream or cry, just turned pale as snow and stood there wiping her hands on her apron.

We all looked at Butte, lying motionless on that mule, arms and legs hanging down into the dirt. Not a movement. Not a whisper. Then all of a sudden he hiccupped, giving up a whole lot of river water and most of his breakfast. The miners cheered and shoved each other and passed around a bottle of whiskey, which even Brother Claymore took a drink from, him apparently not being the kind of preacher to deny an occasional sip of liquor to a man, even himself.

Mama stopped wiping her hands, put Butte to bed with cobwebs and brown sugar on his cuts, and thanked Brother Claymore over and over for his help. "Don't thank me, Sister Whipple," boomed Brother Claymore between sneezes and sips of whiskey. "God Himself reached down and plucked your boy from the jaws of death."

All by myself in the kitchen, I took a deep breath. I was relieved that Butte was all right and grateful to Brother Clyde, but mostly I was pleased. If Mama didn't trust and admire Brother Clyde now that he'd saved Butte's life, she never would. Massachusetts was just around the bend!

But I rejoiced too soon. The miners, sitting outside and finishing that bottle of whiskey, decided that God might have saved Butte, but it was Brother Clyde who had flung himself into the river. "The man is a hero," said Amos Frogge between hiccups. "An honest-to-Godfrey, ding-dong, real-life hero, and I for one aim to go to his prayer meeting and listen to what he has to say." The others agreed with varying degrees of reluctance, and the Gent went in to tell Brother Clyde that they'd all go to his prayer meeting and how was next Saturday.

I was desolate. A prayer meeting would likely mean followers, and followers would mean Brother Clyde wouldn't be a failure and go home, and I was doomed to live in Lucky Diggins until my skin shriveled and I looked like something out of a story by Edgar Allan Poe.

Saturday morning Jimmy Whiskers helped Mr.

Scatter clean up the saloon. People brought benches from their kitchens to line up in front of the bar that Brother Clyde would use as a pulpit. Prairie and Sierra gathered wildflowers, and the Gent turned all the paintings of scantily clad ladies and the "Scatter said it: No credit!" signs toward the wall.

When the sun was high in the sky, people began to gather from up and down the river. I had baked twenty pies, planning to sell to the crowds coming to the meeting. Once again I would have to earn my own fare to Massachusetts.

The Flagg girls showed up from their digs across the river. I had never seen them up close, they being skittish as wild things. Lizzie looked to be my age, perhaps a bit nearer fourteen, and Ruby Ramona was a little mite with braids that stuck straight out from her head. Both were skinny and dirty, smelling of the squalor and the critters they lived with.

The townsfolk were none too friendly toward the Flagg children, their drunken father, or the mother, said to be a lunatic. When the girls started toward my pies, Leo Mack, Poker John Lewis, Billy Parker from the restaurant, and some others began howling like coyotes and throwing pinecones at them. The Flaggs may have been dirty and stupid and crazy, but folk were there for a prayer meeting. Seemed to me the occasion called for more seemly behavior. Sometimes I can't figure people.

Mama and Butte and I tried to protect the pies, but every one of them was crushed in the general bumping and shoving, so finally I gave a free piece of squashed pie to everyone—except Lizzie and Ruby Ramona, who got chased away, and Bernard, who took one look at the unfriendly red faces and left.

After that we crowded into the saloon-turned-house-of-God. A number of the miners called "Howdy, little sister" to me as they pushed and fought their way to the best seats.

People were clapping their hands and stomping their feet when Brother Claymore finally came in, raised his arms in the air, and boomed, "I feel the holy fire start to burn!

"Like Moses," he shouted, "I came a stranger to this strange land, and you gave unto me the right hand of fellowship, hallelujah. So now I extend *my* hand to *you*—join me, brothers and sisters, in making this new land a new Jerusalem, a land where the righteous flourish and the wicked are sent down, where men are praised for their hard and honest labor, their clean and sober ways, serving—"

"Speaking of serving, Preacher, I'll have a whiskey," someone yelled.

"You may laugh now, brother, but wide is the gate to Hell. Do not flounder in the mire of sin. Reject the lure of Satan, for it is the food—"

"Food here! A thick juicy steak!" called someone.

"And fresh peas!" added another.

"And chocolate cake," I shouted, deliberately avoiding Mama's disapproving eyes. If the prayer meeting erupted into rowdiness and merriment, Brother Clyde might still be toting me back east.

Suddenly a shot rang out and silence fell. Brother Claymore stood with his pistol smoking in his hand. "I trust I have your attention now." He sure did. "Remember, brothers, Hell is never full. Satan always has a place for you," and suddenly the big man began to cry and groan and wail. "I feel the fires, the fires of Hell, licking at my feet!" His great voice sang out like the cathedral bells the Hunchback rang as he died for love of Esmeralda. In spite of myself I was moved.

First the miners sat in embarrassed silence, and then some people began to cry and wail along with him. Then we all were shouting and singing regardless of what we believed or did not believe. While some sang "Amazing Grace" or "Hail, Columbia," others bellowed "Buffalo Gals," "Turkey in the Straw," and "From Greenland's Icy Mountains." Pleased at the cacophony, for I was sure it meant the prayer meeting was falling apart, I sang "Home, Sweet Home" with all the fervor I could muster.

Then the Gent took his fiddle and Rusty his mouth harp. As they played, we sang to the tune of "Oh Susanna":

"Oh California,
   That's the place for me.
   I'm off to Sacramento
   With my washbowl on my knee."

Everyone sang especially loud when they got to the word "California," except for me. I sang "Massachusetts" instead, just as loud as I could.

Brother Claymore made ready to pass his hat, saying: "All those who wish to lie down in everlasting darkness may leave; the rest stay and be counted," but I didn't feel threatened. You had to know that Brother Claymore's God would never really send anyone to Hell. He might pinch your cheek or give you a licking for something real bad, but eternal damnation? Never.

Except for Amos Frogge, the congregation slipped away, some to the card parlor, some to a whiskey bottle, others to the back of the saloon, where a number of fights were already starting, and us into the cool spring evening, fragrant with the smell of pines and so quiet after the frenzy inside.

When Brother Clyde came back to the boarding house, I asked, "Are you a shepherd with sheep now, Brother Clyde?"

"One sheep, Miss Lucy. Brother Amos has chosen the path of righteousness."

"Only one?" I felt almost guilty at my pleasure in his

failure. "Then I reckon you'll be leaving here soon for the old states."

"Not hardly, Miss Lucy! Praise the Lord, this is my beginning. A soul saved is a soul saved. Thank you, Jesus!" And he fell to his knees right there and started talking to God.

Doomed. I stayed up late, writing to Gram and Grampop by the light of a candle stub, the sound of Brother Clyde praying soft on the air.

Another plan of mine to get out of Lucky Diggins has come to nothing. Maybe I should have prayed at the meeting for God to help me, but I was so busy trying to sink Brother Clyde that I didn't even think of it.

Everyone else had such a good time singing, as if they all had a home in Lucky Diggins and they were content. Brother Clyde said he was a stranger in a strange land, but I think it is me. There is no place for me here. If I cannot come home to you, I will just wither away into dust and let the wind blow me back to Massachusetts.

I sighed and burned the letter in the candle flame. No use vexing Gram and Grampop. That night I fell asleep restless with sadness and unnamed longings. I had a dream. My pa was not dead. He was lost in the mountains of California. I woke up with my face wet.

CHAPTER TWELVE

Summer 1851

In which I celebrate Independence Day

Butte never completely recovered from his near drowning, as if the river water had done something to his innards. He didn't go back to work on the river but mostly slept or sat in the sun and tried to swallow all that Mama was pushing him to eat. To get away from her broths and tonics, he took over the hunting, sitting on the stump and shooting those rabbits and squirrels foolish enough to invade Prairie's garden. Since he was a much more willing hunter than I, and a better shot, we had more meat that summer and fewer suppers of that tough and stringy beef from the south we called sheet-iron steaks. But things were tight without Butte's wages, and in my pickle crock there were still more cobwebs than gold.

Come July, Lucky Diggins prepared to celebrate the first Independence Day for the new state of California. There were to be fireworks, a picnic, music, speeches, and me, my mind on Massachusetts, selling pies.

July fourth dawned hot enough to fry an egg on a bald man's head, if there had been an egg to spare. Butte was poorly, coughing and spitting and sitting with one hand to his chest, so he stayed at home with Mama. Prairie, Sierra, and I went down to the river, where some canvas awnings were set up. Everyone in town was there, as well as those miners from farther off who thought celebrating this day more important than striking it rich. The Gent fiddled and Mr. Scatter played the squeezebox and Milly from the saloon sang "The Boy I Left Behind Me" and "Maryland, My Maryland" until we all were heartily sick of them. Belle Scatter and her lawyer beau said they'd be happy to watch Prairie and Sierra until dark, "for practice," Belle said, and giggled.

So I found a shady tree, spread a cloth, arranged my pies on it, and sat back to make my fortune. I had been sitting quite a while, fanning flies away and listening to the sounds of celebration—singing, fighting, gunshots, and the imperious voice of Prairie organizing the miners into a game of Ant'ny Over—when Bernard Freeman came by. He bought a slice of pie and said he thought he'd spend the day up on Ranger Creek: "Best I get out of town before the drinking starts. Seems like

I always get in trouble when white folks been drinking too much." I gave him another slice of pie for free.

Nobody else bought pie. There was a long line for watermelons, which Bean Belly Thompson had brought in from the valley and was selling for a dollar each. Even warm, I reckoned, those melons would taste awful good on a hot day, and I watched enviously.

"Take something in trade for a slice of pie?" a voice behind me asked. It was Lizzie Flagg. Her brown hair was matted and dusty, dirt and scratches and mosquito bites marked her face, and her skinny arms and legs were dark with bruises. A tattered buckskin tunic left big holes where pieces of Lizzie showed through.

But Lizzie looked at me with eyes as shiny as seed pods, the most beautiful, observant, intelligent eyes. It was the beatingest thing! There was a human being in there. And she was talking to me.

"Need thirteen cents a slice," I said.

Lizzie Flagg sat right down. "See what I have to trade." She held out a dirty hand. On it, sitting there like it was tamed, was a dragonfly, green and silver and a spot of startling gold that glowed in the sunshine. She had it tied by a piece of thread. When she moved her hand, it flew but, caught by the thread, could only fly in frantic circles around her head. "You can fly it till it drops dead and then pin it to your wall. The colors is so purty in the sun."

"I will give you a small slice of pie for the dragonfly,"

I said, reaching out a finger and tentatively touching a soft wing. Lizzie likely didn't have thirteen cents anyway, and the dragonfly was glorious. "It's so beautiful."

Lizzie's face lit. "You think this is beautiful? Give me the pie and then I'll show you someplace special. Where I found the bug. Everything is beautiful there."

"I can't leave until I sell all the pies."

"Come on," she said, pulling me by the hand. "You can sell them when we get back."

Overwhelmed by Lizzie's enthusiasm, I gave her a slice of pie. While she ate, creek plum juice dripping down her face, I covered the pies from the flies and then let the dragonfly go. It flew away, the summer sun glinting off its wings.

"Why'd you do that?" Lizzie asked. "I ain't givin' the pie back."

"No matter," I said. "Pa never would let us keep wild things. And Mama says they eat, same as people, and she already has enough mouths to feed."

We climbed up out of the ravine, past a stand of young pines with their cones just starting to open, and over a rise. As I was getting so hot and droopy I thought I would perish, Lizzie said, "Here."

"Here" was a meadow in a clearing surrounded by trees. The meadow was filled with wildflowers, white, yellow, gold, orange, striped, dotted, small, large, and in between. Then Lizzie clapped her hands, and the wildflowers took to the air. Butterflies! Yellow with black and red, black splashed with orange, white and pink and blue. They were everywhere, flying and landing, covering entire branches of trees.

"Fairyland," I said.

"What's that?"

"You know, where fairies live."

"What's fairies?"

"You know, fairies, like elves and brownies."

"What are they?"

And so we spent Independence Day lying in a meadow like two pups in a basket, while I told Lizzie Flagg about fairies and elves and brownies. And the Count of Monte Cristo and the kind and beautiful Rebecca. If we lay real still, the butterflies would land on us so that we too seemed covered with wildflowers until we'd laugh and the butterflies would swarm back into the air.

Lizzie in return told me about her family, living off the land and eating only wild things, fruits and herbs and meat. "My pa is a drinkin' man, and mean. The rest of us can take it, but a few years back Ma jist stopped talkin', so feared was she of sayin' the wrong thing and gettin' smacked with his fist or his boot. She ain't crazy or stupid, jist hidin', I reckon."

I'd heard people complain about Linus Flagg when he'd been drinking, but I never thought he was such a bad egg that he'd beat on Mrs. Flagg and his own children. If Pa were alive, I thought, he'd fix Mr. Flagg's flint for sure!

Picking at a scab on her ankle, Lizzie continued. "The boys mostly live outside—hard to tell them from critters sometimes—but I stay, mostly for Ruby Ramona and Ma."

"Can't anybody do something?" I asked. "The sheriff maybe, or Brother Claymore?"

"It's our business. Someday we will do something."

Lizzie looked grim, and I was glad to change the subject. I told her about Robinson Crusoe, who lived off the land like the Flaggs, and she told me how to cook a wood rat, braid a slip-noose snare, and make a whistle out of bird bones and a deer-hoof rattle. We jawed away the afternoon.

I was surprised at what good company Lizzie was, her not knowing about books or anything, although I couldn't imagine what Essie and Opal would make of her. Shoot, I thought, Lizzie is here and they're not. Finally, hot and tired and satisfied, we started back down.

We arrived at the river to find the pies gone and a note: "Little sister, we et yer pies. They was good." And in one empty tin was enough dust for twenty pies, which meant I could buy a watermelon for myself and one for Butte, give Mama some dust, and still have some to put in my pickle crock! I was plumb rapturous.

Lizzie and I sat against a tree slurping the melon, letting the warm juice run down our chins. Leo Mack scratched a friction match across the seat of his pants to light the firecrackers and instead set his rump on fire.

He hopped around like a frog on a griddle until Jimmy knocked him to the ground and rolled him in the dust. Finally the firecrackers were lit, and we screamed joyfully at the noise. Amos Frogge climbed a tree, fired his pistol, shouted "Three cheers for the Declaration of Independence," and fell out of the tree. Jimmy slung Amos over his shoulder, and all the miners went to the saloon.

I carried the melon home to Mama and Butte, stopping every few feet to rest my arms. Seems to me God made a big mistake when He failed to put handles on watermelons.

The rest of the night I spent dosing Prairie and Sierra with spruce tea and sugar to combat the effects of too much watermelon. Mama said it appeared Belle Scatter could use a darn sight more practice watching babies.

CHAPTER THIRTEEN

SUMMER 1851

*In which I learn about living and leaving
and letting go*

Butte came home from hunting one day with a young injured raccoon. She obviously had gotten the worst in a fight, for her tail was missing and her back legs were chewed up some. I washed her sores and put cobwebs on them to stop the bleeding. Mama sighed and said Butte could keep her until she got well. That shows how sick Mama thinks he is, I thought with sudden terror.

Butte made the raccoon a cage of stout twigs. We called her Cora. When she improved, Butte wanted to let her go but I wouldn't, fearing the woods out there were not safe, what with bears and Indians and hunters. Next time the raccoon might not be so lucky. "Cora is better off right here with us, thank you very much," I told him. Pa might not have approved, but Cora stayed, getting well and getting bigger and getting mighty restless in that cage.

My pies turned out to be such a success at the Independence Day picnic that Mr. Scatter ordered ten each day to sell. Soon I was able to take some of the money and hire Lizzie Flagg to help roll crust and cook fruit. Mama said Lizzie was so dirty you could plant potatoes on her neck and not to let her near a pie. I helped Lizzie wash in the laundry tub and Mama gave her an old smock to wear. Lizzie looked a little like a weasel in a dress, but she sure smelled better.

"Never knew a Flagg could be so pretty," Butte said. Lizzie spit at him between her teeth.

Each day that summer Butte was worse. He coughed something awful, got real feverish, and sometimes seemed plumb out of his head. Mama fed him on slippery elm tea and onions boiled with honey, but all her tending did no good. He was so poorly in August that he had to give up hunting, and Lizzie took that over. I went with her sometimes, but I feared a bullet would bounce off the trees and rocks and come back and kill me like it did the bear in "The Ballad of Rattlesnake Jake." Dying was on my mind.

When he was well enough, Butte mostly sat by the cook fire and whittled axe handles and butter paddles, which I sold to Mr. Scatter along with the pies. What with buying supplies, paying Lizzie, and giving what I could to Mama, my pickle crock grew no fuller. Massachusetts might as well have been China.

One day when I was reading to him from *The Castle of Otranto,* Butte interrupted. "Lucy, do you ever think about dying?"

"Sure I do, all the time. I think about being shot by outlaws or eaten by a grizzly . . ."

"No, I mean just dying, piece by piece, feeling yourself dying a little bit at a time. You know how when your shoes get real wet, you put them on the stove and steam rises from them and pretty soon they're dry? Well, I feel like that, as if the life is drifting out of me like steam rising from wet shoes."

I shivered, although my face grew hot. I wasn't ready to admit Butte might not make it. "Don't be foolish. You're not dying. You're not even twelve yet."

He leaned back and closed his eyes. "I ain't scared though," he said, and I could see him trying not to be. "I figure I ain't never had a chance to do nothing worth going to Hell for."

"You're not dying," I repeated, knowing no other way to comfort him, or myself, and we sat then in a silence broken only by the constant ringing of hammer on anvil from Amos Frogge's blacksmith's shop.

July and August were hot and dry as a cookstove. The ground cracked, the rivers dried up, and I was homesick for Massachusetts summer rain. There being no water, the miners had to break rock to look for gold instead of washing it out of the gravel. Many of them just gave up and went to the saloon or to Sacramento or even back home.

Nights were too hot for sleeping, which was just as well since no one with ears could have slept for the noise of Cora tearing at her cage and Butte coughing.

So many people turned up kind. Bean Belly Thompson brought from Sacramento a bottle of "Dr. Lippincott's Celebrated Lung and Nerve Tonic With Sarsaparilla, Garlic, Pennyroyal, Verbena, and Elecampane Root, Effective Against Disorders of the Lung, Hysteric Affection, and the Bite of a Mad Dog" and wouldn't take a penny for it. It didn't help Butte. Snowshoe Ballou brought some elk clover root that Hennit sent. It didn't help either.

Mr. Scatter heard there was a doctor in Skunk Valley, so Jimmy Whiskers and his mule, Arabella, went to fetch him. It took three days, during which only Mama's hope kept her and Butte going.

The Skunk Valley doctor was near as young as me, with a skinny, spotted face. When he saw Butte, he grew so pale that his spots stood out like poppies in the sand.

"I ain't really a doctor," he whispered. "Pulled a few teeth and tended cuts and bruises with some salve my mother gave me for sunburn. Hog's grease and cowslip flowers. But this boy looks real sick, and I ain't no real doctor."

"You are as useless as a wart on a hog's bottom!" Jimmy hollered, and threw him out the door. The boy left, Butte got no better, and Mama got sadder and quieter, as if all her hope had ridden out of town with the boy who was no doctor. Jimmy and Arabella set out for Marysville or Sacramento or San Francisco, or "even, bygod, all the way to Boston," he said, in search of a real doctor. Mama let him go, but she didn't hold out hope for his coming back in time to help Butte.

Prairie and Sierra and I took turns feeding Butte the peppermint tea Mama made and the awful-tasting herb tonics Lizzie brewed up. He didn't talk about dying in front of Mama and the little girls, but when we were alone, he had a lot of questions: Would he see Pa and Golden like the preachers said? Would he see Jesus? Would he see anything or just lie in a hole in the ground while rain leaked in? I had few answers for him.

"Law, Butte, how would I know, never having been dead? Seems to me anyone who'd know isn't around to tell about it. What I'd hope is that all the good things preachers tell us about Heaven and angels and seeing God are true, and all the bad things aren't. I reckon it's hot enough around here without having to worry about Hell, too."

Once he asked, "What will happen to you without me? You're all girls and not even a little boy to be man of the family." He thought a minute and then said, "I think the Gent is sweet on Mama. If—"

"We don't need the Gent. If you were to die, and you're not, Mama and me could take care of this family."

"Maybe you could at that. You got more guts than you think." He grinned. "Maybe everything will turn out."

Brother Clyde came back from bringing the word of God to other towns and camps. He sat with Butte, telling him about God's heavenly kingdom and resting in Abraham's bosom. As Brother Clyde talked in his great ringing voice, Butte's fears seemed to leave him much the way he said his life was: like steam from wet shoes. When Brother Clyde assured him that in Heaven even a boy could be a ship's captain, Butte smiled.

One night Butte lay in an awful silence, no strength left even to cough. Mama, Prairie, Sierra, Brother Clyde, the Gent, and I all sat around his bed. I prayed silently that he would make a sound, even choke or moan, so I would know he was still alive.

Suddenly he opened his eyes wide. "Lucy," he said. "Phlegm cutter."

"What?"

"Phlegm cutter. The forty-ninth word for liquor." He closed his eyes again. That was the last we ever heard him say.

The morning we buried Butte, Jimmy Whiskers came back with a peevish, glowering doctor tied to his mule. While Jimmy helped us dig a hole, that doctor got free and took off, running all the way to San Francisco, I'd guess.

Butte was buried upriver in a meadow with his whittling knife. As Bernard Freeman shoveled the dirt over Butte in his canvas blanket, I dropped a paper in beside him. *Tarantula juice*, it said. Number fifty. Took me a long time asking around town that morning to find it.

I sat afternoons holding on to Cora, crying until her fur was damp. It got harder and harder to stuff Cora back into her cage, but I needed more than ever to keep her.

Prairie and Sierra cried, too, but not Mama. Mama's mouth got harder and her eyes got sadder and she skinned her hair back even tighter, but she did not cry. I watched this woman who looked a little less like Mama every day and grew frightened. I would not let Mama go. What Mama did, I did. Where Mama sat, I sat. Where Mama went, I went, my hand tangled in her apron and my eyes on her face.

"California Morning Whipple, what do you think you are doing besides driving me crazy and keeping me from working?" Mama snapped finally. "Go and make yourself useful."

"I'm afraid, Mama," I told her, tears sliding down my face again. "The world is so dangerous and everybody dies—Gramma Whipple and Pa and Golden, Ocean, and now Butte. I got to hold on to you or I'll die. Or you will."

Mama's face suddenly grew gray and wrinkled, as if she had turned a hundred years old. "Have I done wrong, dragging you children to this wild place where there is not even a doctor? Oh God, would Butte be alive if . . ."

"Mama, don't. It's not your fault. Pa and Golden died in Massachusetts. People die everywhere. It's not your fault. People die."

Mama sniffed. "Listen to you, lecturing me for a change." She patted my cheek. "You and me are so different. Me always looking ahead, face to the west. And you looking behind, at what you had and loved. And lost." Mama looked at me as if seeing me for the first time.

"I just want us all to be safe."

"I guess there is no safety anywhere, except in God's abiding love and your own two feet. We just got to trust in both."

"Butte trusted and he's dead."

"And when you see God, you can ask Him why. Until then . . ." Mama sighed, and for a minute I could see the old Mama in her face. "Until then, I guess all we got is God and each other and our own selves no matter where we are. It's a hard world all right, but you got to stand on your feet and face it." She untangled my hand from her apron, sat me on her lap, and we both cried some. After, we felt better.

That night as I lay awake listening to Cora tearing at

her cage, I thought about what Mama had said. I had pains in my stomach, and my head, and my heart. Finally, sighing, I got out of bed.

The night was warm as day, with the smell of pines and dust and cook fires that had become so familiar. I opened Cora's cage and let her out. The little raccoon tore off into the woods without one look back, never a glance to show she knew I had saved her and loved her and mourned her leaving.

Dear Gram and Grampop,

Butte is dead. He was eleven years old, could do his sums, and knew fifty words for liquor. I didn't know it but I loved him.

The next spring I saw a raccoon family drinking from Buck Creek near the butterfly meadow. The female had two babies and no tail. She looked safe and happy. She did not look up when I called her Cora.

CHAPTER FOURTEEN

*In which Mr. Flagg comes to a bad end
and is not mourned*

September came, hot and still, and the remaining miners had to move farther upriver to find diggings that weren't already dug out, leaving behind them deep pits, bare hills, and piles of gravel. They had to dig deeper holes and wash more dirt, which meant they needed more water. Soon the land was crisscrossed with ditches and tunnels and flumes bringing water from here to there and there to here, all for washing dirt. We diverted some of that water our way and had less trouble with withering crops and thirsty mules, and I didn't have to carry water such long distances for drinking and washing. With the boarders working so far away, no one came home for noon dinner, and I had more time to myself for reading and writing letters, for making pies and money.

In her mourning, Mama paid little attention to what I did, or Prairie or Sierra. The boarding house was neglected, the miners ill fed. Although Mama was always there, in her heart she was out in the meadow with Butte, and those of us left behind felt lonely.

I took to tagging along with Lizzie as she checked her father's traps for critters. Thinking of Cora on her own in the woods, I begged Lizzie to let the animals go if they were not dead, but she just blasted them with her father's Springfield rifle. "Varmints is varmints," Lizzie said, "and good for nothin' but shootin', though some do make fine eatin'." Lizzie would skin the critters right there, put the fur and edible parts in her hunting sack, and rebait the traps with the rest. How different, I thought, from Bernard Freeman, who would not eat bacon even when he was hungry, and how odd of me to admire them both.

As we wandered, Lizzie and I gabbled like turkeys. I told Lizzie about Butte and how he was as a little boy, about Golden and Pa, Gram and Grampop, and Cousin Batty, about school, county fairs, Massachusetts, and the pickle crock. "As you know it is my heart's desire to return to Massachusetts," I said one day. "How about you? Do you have a heart's desire?"

"Seems to me," said Lizzie, "I have about all a body

needs." She paused and chewed on her lip. "Well, maybe if Pa would quit hittin' . . ." Sometimes Lizzie was covered with bruises, but that was the one thing she wouldn't talk about.

Lizzie told me about the salmon that used to crowd the river before the miners arrived and turned the water to mud "too thick to drink and too thin to plow," about the Indians decked in condor feathers dancing their prayers, about grinding manzanita berries and skinning porcupines and smoking the leaves of the wild nicotiana plant.

She taught me how to look at the trees. "They're not all just trees, Luce. They're oaks and firs and cedars and pines. Look here at the pines. Even they are all different. I call this one scaly pine because of the scaly look of the bark. And this one with the bark that looks like fungus I call mushroom pine. Here's smooth pine and there is mighty pine, the biggest."

In this way I learned the names of California things: miner's lettuce, shooting stars, duckweed, thimbleberry, skunkbush, needlegrass, checkerbloom. I didn't know if they were true names or Lizzie's. It didn't seem to matter.

We saw a bobcat rolling in catmint, looking for all the world like a giant kitten, and a hawk with a rabbit in its claws. Once we climbed all morning and came upon a bee pasture, ankle deep in flowers and miles wide, a meadow planted and tended by bees. There were wild rose and bramble and clover, yellow, purple, and pink, the air buzzing with the sound of bees and sweet with fragrance. We lay in the pasture awhile but after a few stings moved on, leaving it to the bees. I never found it again but never forgot it.

On the way back through the woods, Lizzie and I saw an Indian girl, hair matted and dirty, face black with dirt or ashes or bruises. She stumbled as she passed us, and I reached out a steadying hand.

"No," said Lizzie. "Let her be. She ain't hurt. She most likely just turned woman and can't wash or comb her hair or talk to nobody for a few days. She's prob'ly just goin' to piss in the woods."

"Turned woman? You mean her bleeding come on?" I asked, my cheeks on fire. "Why do they send her away for that?"

"She needs to be alone to have her dreams." Lizzie shrugged. "It's what they believe. Like we believe a bleeding woman sours milk and snaps fiddle strings."

"I don't believe that. Nobody does. It's just a monthly illness."

"And I suppose you don't make a stew of pigweed and snakeroot to ease it?"

"No, we just lie down in darkened rooms."

"That something you learned in Massachusetts?" asked Lizzie. "Boy, it sure must be a peculiar place. You do at least know it has something to do with babies?"

I blushed again. "I know that . . . but not exactly

125

what. Anyway, it doesn't really matter to me because I can't imagine myself courting and marrying and having babies and all that."

"I ain't gonna mess with it either. I have enough trouble and bruises from my Pa."

While we were talking, the Indian girl passed again, her eyes on her bare feet. I thought she looked the kind to wink at us if she were allowed.

That was the last time Lizzie and I wandered for a while. The next morning Jimmy Whiskers came running into town, red faced and breathless. Said he was sinking a shaft and came upon Linus Flagg, "lying at the bottom of the hole, dead as a can of corned beef." Snoose McGrath went to fetch the deputy from over at French Bar.

While we waited for them to get back, the news spread through Lucky Diggins fast as a fire through dry grass. Everyone was right curious to see the body, so we hiked out up the river and over a rise to Moon Creek to pay our respects to the former Mr. Flagg. Then we all hiked home, some merry and grateful for an outing, some somber thinking about death and all. I shed a few tears, but not for Mr. Flagg—for Butte, who never drank or beat on anybody and didn't deserve to lie dead at the bottom of a hole.

I thought I could be of comfort to Lizzie, me having lost my pa, too, but Lizzie didn't come to hunt, bake pies, or go wandering. No one saw any of the Flaggs, except for what remained of Linus. Jimmy said they were most likely holed up like wild things, waiting and sorrowing, and just to let them be.

The miners mostly stayed in town and mended shirts and pants. No one dug or shopped or planted. The air was hot and still, as if the whole world were holding its breath until the deputy came.

Then on Friday he appeared, a short, fleshy man with spidery lines on his nose and cheeks, who frowned and grumbled as if Lucky Diggins was the last place, next to Hell, he wanted to be on a hot October day, and it probably was. Everyone hiked back to Moon Creek. The hot weather had caused Mr. Flagg to smell something fierce, so no one but the deputy got very close.

"Been shot," said the deputy.

"Shot . . . shot . . . shot" echoed along the line of those watching.

"Dead a week or two," he added.

"Week or two . . . week or two . . . week or two," the watchers muttered.

The deputy did his detecting: "You seen anything?"

First fellow: "Nope."

The deputy spit and moved on to the next fellow. Didn't seem like he was working too hard.

After a day or so of this and about a hundred of my whortleberry pies, he rode over the river and came back with Mrs. Flagg. Everyone gathered in front of the saloon to see what was going on.

"Excuse me, ladies and gents," said the deputy, "I have broke the case" (meaning Mrs. Flagg agreed she shot her husband) "and I must take Mrs. Flagg to the lockup" (meaning the storeroom in back of the saloon) "until we can convene a jury" (meaning twelve men all sober at the same time) "and have us a trial."

Mama and I took hot soup over to the saloon for Milly, who was ailing. Several men were there setting up for the trial. "Mama," I said, "couldn't we help Mrs. Flagg get a little cleaner and less shabby? I don't think she'd want everyone looking at her the way she is now."

Billy Parker, overhearing, spat and said, "You can put a bow tie on a pig and call him Maurice, but he's still a pig."

Bristling at that and the laughter that followed, I muttered under my breath all the way back to the boarding house: "I should have said, 'Handsome is as handsome does,' or 'A loud voice bespeaks a vulgar man.' I should have said 'A tongue is worth little without a brain.' I should have said . . ."

It wasn't until we reached home that I thought of the right thing to say.

"Mama . . ."

"Leave me be. It don't matter what she wears."

"But Mama, listen. You always listen to Gram, and Gram says, 'It's not only fine feathers that make a fine bird, but it sure don't hurt.'"

At that Mama almost smiled. "Well, look at you. You're getting mighty good at standin' up to me lately."

Gram also said, "Grief don't benefit the dead if it injures the living," but I knew better than to say that to Mama.

We got Mrs. Flagg from the saloon and gave her a bath. Clean, Mrs. Flagg proved to have curly red hair, not greasy brown, and a whole lot of scars and bruises, which Mama clamped her lips tight to see. In my old blue dress, Mrs. Flagg looked young and pretty except for her sad eyes.

Benches were set up in the saloon for the jury: miners who were more curious than greedy for gold, and Mr. Scatter, Amos Frogge, Billy Parker, and Poker John Lewis. Lizzie and Ruby Ramona and the Flagg boys stood at the edge of the crowd. Lizzie looked closed off and silent, as if she had climbed inside herself and blown out the lamp.

Mama did not go. She said the poor woman had enough to contend with without a gaggle of no-accounts goggling at her. So Mama didn't hear about the trial and the outcome until supper, when Jimmy Whiskers told her all about it.

"That ole fat deputy was sweating like a cheese in the sun. Mops his face and asks Mrs. F. did she shoot Flagg? She says not a word but just nods.

"'Guilty!' cries the deputy, banging his shoe on the table, but Scatter up and hollers, 'Now hold on.' He looks at Mrs. F.

"'Did you shoot Linus?' She nods again. 'Why?' She

shrugs. 'What was he doing just before you shot him?'
Mrs. F., she says nothin', but little Ruby Ramona calls
out, 'He was beatin' on her with a sycamore stick.'

"'Your honor,' booms Scatter like he was talking to
someone in Marysville, 'everyone here knows what a
mean son of a gun Flagg was when he was drinking and
how he beat up on the missus with every drink. I say
she shot him in self-defense.'

"'In the back?' asks Billy Parker. No one had an
answer for that, and it appeared that those Flaggs were
going to lose their ma as well as their pa. Why, I felt so
low I could of rid horseback under a snake.

"Then someone, smart as a whip and twice as sassy,
speaks right up and says, 'Maybe it was like in "The
Ballad of Rattlesnake Jake," with the bullet bouncing
all over before hitting Mr. Flagg from behind.'

"Well, she tells the whole story of Rattlesnake Jake
and we all listen and say 'Whoo-ha!' and 'Howdy-do!'
and 'Beat that' until the deputy bangs with his shoe again
and shouts, 'Not guilty, gol durn it, now get me a beer!'"

Jimmy took a deep breath and a swig of his coffee
grown cold. "And it was your daughter, missus, our little sister, that saved that pore lady. You should be right
proud of the girl, right proud."

Mama gave me another one of those looks, like she
never saw me before, and I squirmed. Jimmy beamed at
us both and gave a big smile, splendid with the glimmer
of gold.

"Your gold teeth, Jimmy!" I cried. "You finally got them."

"Yep. From the biggest nuggets I found yet, up in Willow Creek. A doc over to Sacramento City pounded them and wired them in." He smiled again, teeth gleaming in the twilight. "And I can pop them in and out anytime I want." He demonstrated, and there for a minute was the old toothless Jimmy.

They buried Mr. Flagg the next day—"put him to bed," as Jimmy said, "with a pick and shovel." In Brother Clyde's absence, Mr. Scatter said a few words. And I recited some lines I'd learned from a poem of Sir Walter Scott's back in Massachusetts long ago: "He is gone from the mountains; he is lost from the forest." Seemed right for Mr. Flagg the trapper, even if he was a drinking man.

The Flagg boys stayed in the shack across the river, but Mrs. Flagg, Lizzie, and Ruby Ramona moved into a room over the general store and started working for Mr. Scatter. Looked like the pie business was all mine again.

I went over to the store to see Lizzie once she was working.

"Sorry your pa is dead," I said.

Lizzie shrugged. "He was a varmint."

Knowing how she felt about varmints, I've wondered ever since if maybe Lizzie didn't just up and shoot him herself.

CHAPTER FIFTEEN

AUTUMN 1851

*In which the men of Lucky Diggins take to
courting Mama and I take action*

Cholera was ravaging California, and people took
sick and died before anybody even missed them. What
with everyone dead or dying, whole towns disappeared,
like Rocky Bar over the ridge. Jimmy Whiskers said the
trail from Skunk Valley to Sacramento was so thick with
graves, a frog could hop from marker to marker and
never touch the ground.

Lucky Diggins was spared—no one sick, no one
dead. Bean Belly Thompson heard somewhere that the
cholera was caused by eating beans, so folks stopped
eating beans for a while, but slowly we forgot or ran out
of other food or just missed the taste of beans cooked

up with hog fat and molasses, so we started eating beans again, and still no one died. As the weather cooled, life returned to normal.

Prairie and Sierra harvested the last of the corn and laid it in the sun to dry. I spent my mornings getting meat and boiling sheets and such, my afternoons cutting pieces for quilts and making over my aprons for Prairie and Prairie's smocks for Sierra, and my evenings making pies. While they baked, I sat with Bernard teaching him to read until the sky grew too dark. Our favorite books were those about lords and ladies and knights—we finished the last page of *The Castle of Otranto* one day and the next started it all over again— but we read whatever we could get our hands on: newspapers, advertising broadsides, legal announcements, anything with words. Bernard didn't get much practice, for we both loved to hear me read, but slowly he grew from passable to proficient. And what he lacked in accuracy he made up for in fervor, his particular favorite being *Highlights from Shakespeare.*

"Bernard," I asked one evening after King Richard's opening speech, "you ever think about being an actor, like that traveling troupe that's over to Marysville?"

"Folks might let me live here and eat here and work here, but that don't mean I kin do whatever I want. No way nohow they'd let me on a stage."

I blushed, glad that in the dark he couldn't see. "I'm sorry," I said.

"For what? It ain't your fault none."

"I'm sorry for bringing it up, for being so stupid and not paying attention to what life is like for you. I'm sorry you're treated the way you are."

Bernard said nothing.

Mr. Scatter and Snoose McGrath started building a big new kitchen on the boarding house so Mama could feed more boarders. There were Mama and Mr. Scatter together every day, deciding where the kitchen was to be and how many shelves she would need. And there was Mr. Scatter saying, "Why now, you're right, ma'am. How did a purty little thing like you figure that out?" and "Mrs. Whipple, I wouldn't let ole Snoose go a whit further until I got your advice on this."

Poker John Lewis came back from Sacramento with a sack of flower bulbs—yellow daffodil, purple crocus, and iris "the sure-enough color of your eyes, Mrs. Whipple, ma'am." Mama's face shone like the sun as she planted them outside the door of the new kitchen. Then the Gent disappeared for a week. Happens he went to San Francisco on the steamer *Hulda Mae* and returned with a sampler that had "Home Sweet Home" embroidered in colored wool, trimmed with flowers and trees made of human hair. The next week Mr. Scatter showed up with a real glass window for the kitchen and asked Mama, "What, Mrs. Whipple, ma'am, would you like to be lookin' at while your beans are boilin'?"

Belle Scatter had gone and married her lawyer fellow—"Guess this proves there's a lid for every pot," said Mama with a shrug—and now I had marriage on my mind. I feared Mama's suitors were exhibiting more than an outbreak of generosity and good manners toward a poor widow woman, so I watched carefully. Too many lids in Lucky Diggins seemed to be searching for pots.

Dear Gram and Grampop,

It is October and my birthday, but it seems like Mama is getting all the presents. She did make me sweet honey fritters and we had a little party. Lizzie and Ruby Ramona came, and Mr. Scatter, Poker John Lewis, Beppie Parker, the Gent (who brought me Pride *and* Prejudice *from San Francisco), Jimmy, and Bernard because it was my birthday and I insisted. While others danced, I commenced to read and didn't look up until I heard loud angry voices over the sound of the Gent's fiddle. I was afraid they were making trouble for Bernard, but it seems Mama had sat down to rest at the end of the divan we made from sacks of flour and a red plush throw, and Mr. Scatter and Poker John Lewis were arguing over who would sit next to her. The Gent put down his fiddle and tried to slide onto the seat, too, and then all Sam Hill (pardon me) broke loose.*

The Gent shouted to Mr. Scatter, "I don't care a bean if you are the biggest toad in this puddle, I aim to sit here. Not a bean. Not a baked bean. Not a string bean!"

"Vagabond! Rogue! Border ruffian!" were shouted as

well as things Mama would never let me write and tell you.

Suddenly Mama spoke, so quietly that everyone had to shut their pans to hear her and so firmly that everyone listened. "Shame on you, acting like rowdy children! Stop this ruckus or I'll go throw myself in the river." It was as quiet as a tree full of owls. "Now listen to me good. You hounds are sniffing around the wrong dog's tail. I am not hankering to be wooed, pursued, courted, sparked, or any such thing. And I am not in the mood to be marrying anyone. Anyone!" she said, looking directly at Mr. Scatter, the Gent, and Poker John Lewis, still with Mr. Scatter's starched white collar grasped in his fist.

So your daughter is still a widow and life goes on in Lucky Diggins and I am fourteen and near grown, although to most people around here I'm still little sister. I am not fat anymore, am taller than Mama, and my yellow hair is now mostly brown. What I would have liked most for my birthday is to see you, but I thank you sincerely for the ribbons and the warm wool shawl.

Most of the boarders went south or west as autumn deepened, and we rattled around in the boarding house with its big, new kitchen. The Gent hung around the house, and Mr. Scatter and Poker John Lewis came calling frequently. I confessed to Prairie my worries about Mama and her suitors. "Mama says she is of no mind to marry anyone, but what if she changes her mind? What if the Gent or Poker John Lewis promises her something so utterly wonderful that she cannot but say yes?"

"Then she will say yes," Prairie said.

"Do you want someone sleeping and eating in Pa's place? Telling us what to do like he was our pa? Taking up all of Mama's time and attention and leaving none for us?"

Sierra said, "I like the Gent. He would be a good pa."

Prairie, mending socks, added, "Jimmy Whiskers says curly-headed men are industrious and make good husbands."

"Gol durn, rip-snortin' rumhole and cussed, dad-blamed, dag diggety, thundering pisspot," I said later to myself. "Why can't they understand? We got to keep Mama single or we'll lose her." Without Butte to cajole into helping me, I looked for advice where I always looked—in a book. And I found it in an old ballad about the beloved of Clerk Saunders, who wore no shoes or stockings nor combed her hair for seven years in mourning at his death.

"That's it!" I cried. "Oh Mr. Scatter," I would say, "Mama would never ever tell you herself, for it was a sacred private oath, but she has determined not to be courted or wed but to mourn for seven years for my Pa. She wears no gloves or cloaks of fur and will not until the seven years are over." I imagined this being true, and tears for the doomed lovers filled my eyes. Sometimes being so fantastical comes in handy.

I told Mr. Scatter and Poker John Lewis and the Gent and, for good measure, Ripley Gurgins, who was known to be looking for a wife although he was not exactly courting Mama yet. I reckon they believed me, for they came around less and less.

When autumn deepened and even selfless men of God could not sleep outside, Brother Claymore returned and filled up the house with his big laughter. Even Mama took to smiling and laughing again. One morning I chanced upon him seated by the cookstove.

"What the dickens are you doing?"

"Sewing curtains for your mama's kitchen window."

"Sewing? You know how to sew?"

"I figure it's like darning socks—put two ends together and stitch—and I've darned a lot of socks. Damned 'em too, sometimes," he said with a laugh.

There he sat, big hands like hams pushing a tiny needle through rose-sprigged muslin to make curtains for my mama. Seemed like another dog would be sniffing around, and this one had God on his side. I thought to try the Clerk Saunders story on him but decided against it. I couldn't see him swallowing such a tale as easily as Ripley Gurgins, at least without talking it over with Mama. So I just counted on Mama not being in a marrying mood. But Brother Clyde's big hands and merry heart reminded me of Pa, and I found myself smiling at him as I started boiling up the coffee for breakfast.

CHAPTER SIXTEEN

SPRING/SUMMER 1852
In which an ill wind blows nobody good

Ever after I thought of it as the Ice Time, that February and March of 1852 when the snow would not melt and everything green froze and everything frozen was too hard and too treacherous to lift, pick, or walk on. Tents collapsed from the weight of the snow, and those miners who stayed behind for the winter crowded into the boarding house and the saloons. Anything or anybody outdoors overnight was an icicle come morning. Mr. Scatter let Bernard sleep on the floor of the general store in exchange for sweeping and stacking, packing and unpacking, and Brother Clyde's mule, Apostle, moved into the shed Bernard had inherited from Sweetheart.

Food mostly ran out at the end of February, winter usually meaning lean pickings anyway, and we tried to stay alive on potatoes, barley broth, and a kind of bread made from flour and water with a drop of molasses to kill the taste of weevils. Even Mr. Scatter's celebration pickled beets got eaten, and Jimmy said that now he would give twenty dollars in gold for one of those fondly remembered sheet-iron steaks. I was afraid we'd be reduced to eating tallow candles.

Rusty and the Gent went hunting several times but mostly came back empty-handed. One time Rusty returned without the Gent, and we all feared he was lost in the snow. Many hours later here came the Gent, dragging the carcass of a deer. He figured he had pulled that deer near six miles through the snow. While Rusty and Jimmy cut up the meat, Mama rubbed the Gent's feet with snow, for they were frostbit. He soaked them in cold and then hot water; still his toes were dead white and painful for a long time after. But we did eat good for a while.

Lucky Diggins stayed indoors, animals sleeping and dreaming of green meadows, Mama and us sewing quilts and knitting stockings, and the miners entertaining themselves with poker, whist, ninepins, fighting for the last of the salted mackerel, drinking while there was drink, and listening for the arrival of a pack train. "I hear a mule bell," someone would shout, and everyone within hearing would run to the door and look out but see only snow falling, meaning the paths were not clear and the passes were not open and no butter or eggs or whiskey would be coming to Lucky Diggins today.

Folks kept their spirits up any way they could. I had my books, which I turned into plays with Prairie, Sierra, and Jimmy until no one would agree to watch anymore. Mama and Brother Clyde talked Heaven and Hell, argued about sore foot remedies, and danced while the Gent played his fiddle, saying we should pretend he was a whole orchestra and the cookstove a potted plant.

One day, while I sat with a flapjack on my head trying to ease my headache (an old remedy of Gramma Whipple's), Brother Clyde bundled up Prairie and Sierra in all the clothes they could find and took them outside to count snowflakes. When they came in, noses cold and red, Clyde said, "We were almost finished counting when some snow blew in from the west and mixed with what we'd already counted." Prairie just snorted and wiped the steam from her spectacles, but Mama laughed and beamed on Clyde as if she were a hound and he her only pup.

Although most of the folk in Lucky Diggins came from the old states and had suffered through long, harsh winters, we all grew winter weary, this being California and not ordinarily so bitter. I could understand the passion of Prairie who from time to time slipped outside to her garden and scraped away the snow and ice to see and feel and smell the earth and crumble it between her fingers.

141

A thaw came as it always does. The snow turned to mud, and the river to a mass of dark-foamed waves. The sun even came out now and then to tease us with the promise of spring.

One day I pulled on Butte's old India-rubber boots and stepped outside. There was, for the first time since Christmas, no snow. The slush had melted, revealing the streets (for Lucky Diggins had grown to two) piled with gravel mounds, empty bottles, oyster cans, sardine boxes, worn-out kettles, and rusty tools. I looked up as a flock of ring doves, happy to see the pale sunshine, swooped over the town only to be met with pistol and rifle fire. Although I mourned for the soft dead birds, I did enjoy the stews and soups and pigeon pies we turned them into.

By the end of April Lucky Diggins was ready to start living again. The snow was a bad memory, the days warm and dry, the passes sure to open soon. Mama's crocus and daffodil bulbs sent up soft green shoots, promising a riot of flowers if folks would just be patient. Brother Clyde left to go preaching, a jar of Mama's sore-foot remedy tucked in his sack, and a mess of new boarders moved in.

May and June were like summer, hot and still. Grasses and wild berries threatened to overgrow the town, and flowers appeared in the middle of streets and paths, in pits and holes abandoned by the miners, and even on the piles of mule manure thawing in the sunshine. The warm breezes were so welcome after the ice of winter, I ate most of my meals outside, face to the sun, trying to fatten up again. But as the hot days went on, I began to worry. If spring was like this, what would August bring?

The warm breezes turned into hot wind, and there was no more eating outside. There was dirt in our food and our eyes and our mouths. My lips cracked, and my hands, as the hot wind sucked all the juices out of me.

One morning that hot wind grew bolder, blowing like it came directly from Hell, searing our faces and noses and throats. Twigs and dry leaves whipped through the air, several tents blew down, and the Gent's top hat flew right off his head, down the street, across the river, and out of sight, while the Gent stumbled swearing after it. He returned later bareheaded and bad tempered.

Prairie and Sierra were hot and fidgety, so I sat with them under a tree and tried to turn "The Rime of the Ancient Mariner" into a story suitable for youngsters.

"I don't want that story," said Sierra. "Tell me about Pa."

"Well," I said, "Pa was the skinniest man I ever saw, with red hair and a big laugh—"

"Not that, Lucy. You always say that. Tell me something else about him. Were his ears big or small? Did he have freckles? All his teeth? Did you ever see him cry?"

I dumped Sierra roughly off my lap and stood up to shake my skirts and get cool.

"What'd I say to peeve Lucy?" asked Sierra.

Prairie looked up from her mending and said softly, "I think she doesn't remember."

"I do so remember," I said, marching the girls back into the house so Mama could deal with them for a while.

Suddenly the sky grew darkish, and the wind roared with a noise like thunder, blowing under the tents, through the cracks in the cabins, around windows and doors. Something was wrong. I could feel it in my bones. Minutes later I heard the first cries: "Fire! Fire! Fire in the town!"

Jimmy said later that it started in Billy Parker's restaurant when a lantern was blown over and ignited the canvas of the tent kitchen. From there it was blown by the wind to the blacksmith tent, then to the general store, the saloon, and the rest of the town. Tents and cabins and trees exploded into flame. The rows of wooden buildings on the streets caught fire quickly. Their skeletons stood for a while glowing red before tumbling to the ground.

The wind blew the fire through the west side of the ravine, so folks mostly scattered east across the river and up into the trees, carrying whatever we could to safety. Mama brought her coffee grinder and a picture of Pa, Milly her hat with flowers and a bottle of scent. Jimmy Whiskers had his tin plate with breakfast still on it, and Mr. Scatter his canary. I, of course, grabbed my pickle crock and the first book that came to hand. Prairie had a whistle Butte had whittled for her. Bernard could bring nothing of his own, for he carried Sierra.

The air was stifling hot, the sky dark with smoke, and the sun blood red. It was like *The Ancient Mariner* come to life. Covered with cinders and ashes, we stood under the shelter of the trees watching the fire gobble up everything it touched, roaring louder than a train. It took thirty-three minutes by Mr. Scatter's pocket watch for that fire to burn down the town. Took a bit longer for it to reach the tents along the river and then clamber up the ravine into the woods, where it raced away from Lucky Diggins with a deafening roar. But it was many hours before we felt safe enough to come creeping back to see what was left, hoping in our heart of hearts things weren't as bad as we feared.

They were. One wall of Mr. Scatter's saloon and an acre of ashes—that's what was left. Everything else was gone. The saloons, the general store, the smithy were gone. The boarding house and all my books but the one I carried were gone. The town was gone.

We gathered together before the one remaining wall of the saloon. That place had been much more than just a thirst parlor to the folks of Lucky Diggins; it had served as post office, gambling den, dance hall, livery stable, courtroom, church, assay office, social club, and extra bedroom on a number of occasions. Its charred wall was the only familiar thing in town, and, stunned and overwhelmed, we huddled against it for comfort. There were Mr. Scatter and his canary; Mama and Prairie and Sierra and me; Bernard Freeman; Mrs. Flagg with Lizzie and Ruby Ramona; Milly from the saloon; Amos Frogge, the blacksmith; Snoose McGrath, who did odd jobs; Poker John Lewis from the other saloon; Billy and Beppie Parker from the restaurant; King Luke, who ran the supply store; Ripley Gurgins and his pants-wearing, pipe-smoking daughter Nessa, who were prospecting at Owl Creek; Jimmy Whiskers; the Gent; a couple of other miners who had been caught in town when the fire started; and three scared mules.

What were we to do now?

"This town, it's done for," said Amos Frogge.

"It's finished," agreed the Gent.

"It's over."

"Gone."

"Through."

"Kaput."

Defeat and hopelessness were so heavy, I could almost smell them over the smell of burning and ashes and pines. I thought this might be a good time to talk about going home to Massachusetts, but one look at Mama's face shut my mouth fast.

Lizzie was so distressed, she let me hug her. Prairie just stood quiet, her hand in her mouth, while Mama tried to soothe Sierra, who was shaken all to pieces and kept crying about the monster, as if the fire were a roaring red dragon that had devoured Lucky Diggins. Mama kept looking up at the blazing hillsides and muttering about Brother Clyde wandering out there where the fire was. Me? I felt like all the air had gone out of me. Lucky Diggins wasn't much, but until I got back to Massachusetts, it was all the home and safety and certainty that I had. And now it was gone. Everything was gone, and we were stranded in the wilderness with nothing but a few trinkets and the clothes on our backs.

I didn't cry, just sat dry-eyed and stared at the ashes, until I heard Billy Parker, his face red and dangerous, shout at Bernard, "We ain't had but bad luck since you came here, feller. Gold runnin' out, bad weather, now a fire. I think maybe yer a Jonah, bringin' hard times our way."

King Luke and Poker John Lewis came up behind him, muttering and swearing, and I grew afraid. "Mama?"

"Calm down, Miss Lucy," Bernard said. "Words don't hurt nobody none if they just stay words." Bernard started to walk away, but Billy stepped in front of him.

Mama went right up to Billy and grabbed him by his red suspenders. "Don't we have enough trouble with the weather and the wind and the fire?" Mama asked. "Don't you have anything better to do than bait a youngster over things you know ain't his fault? Billy, it was your place where the fire started. I don't see anybody blaming *you*. Go with John and King and see what help you can be instead of trouble. Go. Shoo!" To my amazement, the men went.

"That was right brave, Mama," I said. Bernard nodded slightly in agreement and went off by himself.

"Not hardly," said Mama. "Those ruffians don't have the guts of a rabbit when they're not liquored up."

"Why did you call Bernard a youngster? Isn't he old?"

"Hardly older than you, girl. You mean you never noticed that?"

"Must be the beard makes him look old," I said, "or his sad face." I was a little ashamed that I had never really looked at Bernard as a person but more like a plaything, something I found up by Ranger Creek, called by my father's name, and brought home to play with.

While the men of Lucky Diggins stood and argued about what to do next, we women set about gathering what branches and brush we could for shelter and beds. Whatever the men decided, we weren't going anywhere for a while. The fire had made the trail into Lucky Diggins a tangle of stubble, half-burned branches, and ash. No one was going to be passing over, under, or through that anytime soon.

"How old are you, Bernard?" I asked later, as we

hunted nuts and seeds and spring greens that had escaped the fire to serve as a supper of sorts.

"Don't rightly know, missy. I ain't twenty yet, I know that. Mr. Sawyer, he used to beat all his slaves when they got twenty so's they didn't get any ideas about being grown-up and independent. And I never got that beating."

"You look older. Old, even."

"Mr. Sawyer, he's looking for a young runaway slave. Better I look old. Plenty of time to be young when I'm free."

"Bernard, I was thinking." I looked down and chewed on my lip. "I was thinking, maybe it wasn't right of me to name you, like a doll or a dog or something. You're a man—maybe you should be choosing your own name."

"I agree, missy. I agree. And I'm choosing the name a friend offered. Bernard. I'm proud to have it."

"Mr. Sawyer will never think to look for an old man named Bernard. I guess you're pretty safe here."

"I hope you're right, Miss Lucy."

I smiled. "Just Lucy."

"I hope you're right, Just Lucy." And Bernard smiled, finally smiled. He looked much younger.

That evening was cool and eerie, with the smoke still rising from the ashes with an awful stink and the terrible quiet of a place without birds or squirrels or lizards, without crickets or bees or grasshoppers, a dead place.

We mixed up all the edibles we had found into a sort of stew and tried to eat it. It tasted like ashes. Then, just as it was getting dark, from all along the ravine, from down off those hills and mountains spared from the fire, came rivers of light. The flickering, shimmering rivers all converged at a spot above the ravine and flowed down toward the burned-out town. Everyone watched silently, curious and anxious.

The river came closer and showed itself to be lanterns and torches of branches and tiny pine trees aflame, carried by hairy, dirty, bearded men in flannel shirts and torn pants, men loaded with blankets and tools and bedrolls, onions and coffee and beans. Miners from the hills who had seen the smoke and flames and had come to help, stumbling and tumbling through the pathless mountains, owning little but willing to share.

They put down their bundles and stretched. A couple of the biggest took off their shirts and started chopping scorched trees into logs. Others shoveled ashes out of the way, while some made tents of twigs and branches and threw blankets over. We all stood around and watched for a minute. Jimmy said, "Seems gold's not the only thing of value in California," and started working right along with them. Finally we all did.

In the waning light I saw a movement near the river. "Ma!" I hollered. "Something is there!"

Amos Frogge came over and called out, "Stranger coming. Indian."

I watched the stranger get closer and closer, coming out of the smoke and gloom like some sorcerer or evil spirit. What trouble was coming now? Milly pushed Prairie and Sierra behind her. Poker John Lewis, his face all twisted and ugly, said, "Plug him," and some of the miners pulled their pistols. We waited.

The Indian was buck naked except for a sort of leather apron. Smelling of bear grease and pine, he walked right up to the Gent and began chanting, low and soft and mesmerizing. Suddenly he pulled from behind his back a high silk hat, wet and muddy and a little dented; but there it was, the Gent's hat come home. The Gent clapped it on his head, pounded the Indian on the back, and laughed the only laugh heard around Lucky Diggins all day.

By the light of treetops still on fire, I took the opportunity to see what book I had saved from the fire. It was *The Little Christian's Book of Pious Thoughts.*

Then I cried.

Mama, Prairie, Sierra, and I spent the night huddled close to one another and to the warmth of the embers of what we had lost. In the morning we poked through the smoking ashes to find what we could. In places those ashes were higher than my knees and too hot to touch. But Prairie managed to spy some spoons that had not melted into hunks of tin, a couple of pots, and Mama's cookstove, standing there just as good and proud as ever. Amos Frogge found his tools, though the wooden handles were burned. Mrs. Flagg and Lizzie found some cracked and blackened jugs, and I unearthed the scorched metal frame of the "Home Sweet Home" sampler. There were some unbroken bottles in the saloon and a barrel or two of salted meat in the ashes of the general store. Whenever someone found something good or whole or usable, he would call out, and everyone would cheer.

Scorched bits of paper had settled like snowflakes on the ash heaps and burned stumps. All that was left of my books. A phrase or two here and there was readable: "Friday: Yes, my nation eat mans. . . ." "I now descended my rope ladder and joined my wife and children. . . ." "You jest, Sir Knight. . . ." And ". . . my heart swells when I think of Torquilstone and the lists of Templestowe." I collected the scraps and then, not knowing what else to do, threw them to the winds.

Mama sifted carefully through the remains of the boarding house, looking for something of Butte's. "Seems like he's really gone now," she said to Prairie and me. "Not even a shoe or a shirt left to remind me of him." Mama started to cry, so Prairie let her blow Butte's whistle, and then we all cried, thinking of Butte up in Heaven watching his family standing in the ashes of their home, blowing a whistle to remember him.

CHAPTER SEVENTEEN

Summer 1852

In which Lucky Diggins is down on its luck

Never before or since have I been someplace so quiet. It wasn't only that the birds and frogs and crickets were gone. There were no trees for the wind to whistle through, no rockers to rock, no nails to pound, no singing or hollering or laughing. Although a man and a mule might, with effort and plenty of time, get out of Lucky Diggins and over the pass, no wagon or supply train could get in. We were stranded, with the ashes of all we needed to survive. Every so often I'd reach for something—hairpins, a clean apron, or *Ivanhoe*—and realize it had turned to smoke and ashes, and we were out here in the wilderness with *nothing*. And I'd cry.

I mourned especially for those things that reminded

me of people who were gone: Gramma Whipple's chicken basket that I'd carried pies in, Butte's India-rubber boots, a drawing of Grampop and Rocky Flat, Pa's old straw hat that Mama wore in the sun sometimes. Now that the things were gone, I had only my memories. In the end, I suppose, that's where dead people live anyway, in our memories, but I would have given a dozen eggs and a chocolate cake for Pa's smelly old straw hat.

Jimmy's mule, Arabella, her ears forward and eyes wide open, kept rubbing herself against the saloon wall, so we knew rain was coming soon. Mama, Milly, Mrs. Flagg, Lizzie, Ruby Ramona, and I took the rags and blankets, needles and thread, that those kindly miners had brought us and cut some into capes and coats and sewed some into tents. Jimmy said it was too bad his extra shirt got burned up, for it could have made a tent for our whole family with space left over for a card room and a privy.

Snoose and Jimmy were in charge of shelter, gathering and stacking what hadn't been burned for makeshift houses. Bernard, Prairie, and Sierra gathered brush, greens, and nuts. Amos made nails out of pots that had melted together in the fire, and the Gent tried to cobble together a fiddle sort of thing out of what wood and string he could find. It was like we were on a big town picnic, all of us working together to stay warm and dry and fed, but without the smiles and food and three-legged races.

The middle of June it began to rain, but by then everyone had shelter—a tangle of cabins and lean-tos, unpainted board shacks, and tents of canvas, of blankets, of brush, of potato sacks and old shirts. It looked a lot like the Lucky Diggins I had seen some years before from above the ravine, but smaller, dirtier, poorer, and certainly no prettier.

Snowshoe had been trapped by the fire with Hennit and his people. He came one day with acorn meal and wild greens from the Indians, and the Flagg boys brought meat from time to time. We had enough to eat, though I got mighty sick of rabbit-and-acorn stew, venison-bone soup, and grizzly with beans. I lay on my back sometimes, looking up at the sun, making rhymes about foods I hadn't seen in a goose age and likely would not for a while yet: "Tomatoes, corn, and rutabagas; oyster stew and cheese; fresh milk, butter, pumpkin pie; and lemons, if you please." Made my mouth water and my stomach groan with pleasure and pain.

We reckoned that soon a pack train or something would clear a path through the charred remains of the woods and reach Lucky Diggins. We could then eat a real meal and replace our pots and pans, buckets, linens, bushels of oats and wheat and dried apples. Funny how fast what little we had here in Lucky Diggins began to seem like luxuries.

But we'd need money when that pack train came. I reluctantly gave Mama half my Massachusetts money and buried the other half near the scorched stump. Mama and I gathered pigweed, plums, and acorns to trade for meat and flour. Prairie and Sierra sifted through the ashes of the town for gold dust and nuggets. At night we baked acorn-meal biscuits and doughy little crabapple pies to sell to the miners. Then for a few hours we slept on scratchy brush and branches, dreaming of what we no longer had, of hairbrushes and soap, forks and baskets and table spreads, ribbons and trimmings on caps and hats, flannel, cotton, wool, and featherbeds. Of books and clean paper and pens.

The days were longer now, which made everyone easier, for the remains of the town looked so spooky in the dark, silhouetted against the moon. By day the smell of char and ash was bad enough, but at night it smelled like the depths of Hell, ghostly and evil.

One morning we woke up afloat in mud and soggy ashes. The scorched hills were bare as a baby's bottom, Jimmy said, and with no trees or bushes to hold the ground together, the hillsides had slid down into the ravine. The weather stayed cool and gray, and many of us coughed all night with the damp. The Gent said the rheumatics had got him from standing so often in icy water up to his unmentionables, and he mostly just sat and brooded and strummed on his homemade fiddle.

The town was gone, the game was gone, and the miners were finding that even the far diggings were pretty much worked out, and many of them moved on into the mountains. Others took to digging tunnels, called coyote holes, in the gritty banks of the river; more than one digger was buried in a cave-in, and the rest decided not to risk it. There was talk about breaking the gold out of rocks, but that was beyond the miners' resources. Gloom hung in the air.

Real summer came at last. On a powerful hot day, while I sat with my feet dangling in the tepid shallows of the river, Snowshoe Ballou came by, his big feet stirring up the dust like an unlucky wind. I feared more bad news.

"Saying good-bye, little sister. Moving on." He tipped his hat and turned to go.

"Wait, Snowshoe. Wait. Where are you going and why?"

Two questions—it looked for a moment like they might be too much for Snowshoe, but finally he swallowed hard and answered. "Farther into the mountains. Me and Hennit and his kin. Too many folks around here lately. Done caught all the fish, killed the game, dammed the rivers, cut down the trees, scattered the acorns, then burned it all down. Indians can't live here no more, and neither kin I." He looked up into the woods. "Too bad. Mighty purty country once, afore it was fished and logged and mined to death. Me and Hennit, we got to go. Up there, where is more game and less people."

After this longest speech of his life, he tipped his hat

again and left. I watched him climb up the ravine path to the edge of the woods, where he joined a group of Indians, backs laden with skins and packs and babies. I waved until I couldn't see them anymore.

Walking home, I whispered, "Know many, trust few, always paddle your own canoe." That's what Snowshoe wanted—his own canoe again. I hoped he'd find it.

Then one day Bernard said, "I been helping Mr. Scatter pick through the ashes of his store, and I found this here paper stuffed inside a jug. It's a page from a newspaper back in the old states. See, says here that there are colored men in San Francisco who own their own laundries, restaurants, shops, boarding houses. Help other colored folk, even slaves. Got meeting rooms and a library and everything. You reckon it's true?"

"I reckon so, if it's in the paper."

"I'm thinking maybe I'll go to San Francisco and see can they help me get free of this slavery thing so I don't have to hide from Mr. Sawyer anymore. That's what I'd really like: to be truly free."

"So you have a heart's desire, too."

"Yes, I guess I do at that." He bowed. "Farewell, Lady Isabella."

I curtsied, slow and graceful, almost like a lady. "Godspeed, Prince Alfonso. I hope you have better luck with your heart's desire than I've had with mine."

A week later Bernard Freeman was gone. I knew for

certain I'd rather have him free in San Francisco than a slave back here in Lucky Diggins, but his leaving left a hole in my life.

"Lucy, come sit with me a spell. I want to talk with you," said Mama the day after Bernard left. She sat on our leaf-and-brush bed and patted the place next to her.

Mama sitting down in the middle of the afternoon on a Tuesday? When there was supper to make? "Mama, you're not dying, are you?"

Mama laughed. "No, child. Quite the contrary. I am most wonderfully alive." I looked at her closely. She did look mighty lively, with roses in her cheeks and light in her eyes, and her hair gathered softly at the nape of her neck. "I just want to talk to you."

"What have I not done now?"

"Nothing, Lucy. It's just that . . ." Mama took a deep breath and went on. "We've been seeing for a while now that Lucky Diggins is dying. Folk are moving on, going north, west, back home. Maybe it's time for us to look to moving on, too."

My stomach turned bottom side up. My heart's desire! Home to Massachusetts!

"Clyde, Brother Claymore, has come back," Mama continued. "He prayed on this long and hard and has come to a decision. He'll be going to the Sandwich Islands, to work with the heathens, though Clyde says he thinks there may be more heathens in New York

City than all the South Sea Islands combined." Mama smiled, patting her hair into place. "And he wants us to go with him—you, me, Prairie, and Sierra. So there we will be, heading west again, toward the setting sun, all of us together. Isn't that some news?"

I was horrified. "The Sandwich Islands? Mama, I want to go back to Massachusetts, not to some islands out in the middle of the ocean. Please, Mama, can't we just go home?"

"Well, Miss Lucy, here's how I see it. There's worms in apples and worms in radishes. The worm in the radish, he thinks the whole world is a radish. But not me. I know there is more, more than Massachusetts, more than California. Why, before we left Buttonfields, if I could have seen all the dishes I would wash in California and all the bread I would make and all the sheets I would wash all piled up, I would have lain down and died right there. Now I have a chance to leave the dishes and the sheets and see the apple. And I'm going to take it."

She stopped, smiled again, and said, "There's more. Clyde wants me to go as his wife."

I stared at Mama.

"Well," Mama continued, "what do you think?"

"I think I do not believe what I am hearing. The Sandwich Islands! Marry Clyde Claymore! Mama, you said you were not in the mood to marry anyone!"

"Minds, like diapers, need occasional changing," said

Mama. With that she got up, gave her head and her skirt a shake, and headed for the cookstove.

I ran down to the river, tears pouring down my face. The Sandwich Islands! Someplace more remote and deserted even than here! Uprooted again. Leaving behind what little there was that was dear and familiar! And even worse, Mama getting married! What about Pa, waiting in Heaven for Mama and her married to someone else? How could she?

I flopped onto the riverbank, stuck my feet into the mucky water again, and thought about Pa—Pa holding me tight so I could wade in the ocean without being too scared; Pa and me standing hand in hand, with our coats on over our nightshirts and our heavy snow boots unbuckled, watching the rabbits dance in the moonlight. I recalled the touch of his rough hands and his even rougher beard and remembered him coming home after a time in Boston, and Mama running to him across the field, her face filled with love and longing, and Pa's face . . . Pa's face . . .

I couldn't remember his face! Prairie was right. "I know he had red hair and a bristly beard," I whispered, "but I cannot really see his face. Oh, Pa . . ."

I cried for a spell, and it wasn't until I stopped making weeping noises that I thought I heard Pa's voice talking to me, telling me the way he always did, "Look, California, look.

"Look at your mama," he went on. And I saw again

161

Mama sorting out and throwing out and giving away most of what we owned, leaving memories and dreams and love behind in Massachusetts and carting all of us to this place where she was nearly the only woman and responsible for everything we put in our mouths or on our backs. I saw Mama in her old black dress sewing by candlelight long after I'd gone to bed and fanning the fire in the morning long before I was astir. I saw Mama's face when Brother Clyde brought Butte back, draped over the back of a mule; when she talked to Pa in the moonlight; when she told me about Clyde and the Sandwich Islands and being his wife.

By the time I returned to the boarding house, all worn out from crying and looking and listening, it was suppertime. Mama and Clyde, Prairie and Sierra, were at the makeshift table, grabbing mugs of this and passing platters of that. Sierra was saying, "I think in the Sandwich Islands sandwiches must grow on trees."

Brother Clyde laughed and said, "Almost right, little dearie; they do have breadfruit trees." I walked over to him and pulled his sleeve.

He looked up, big smile on his face and big hands holding a hunk of acorn-meal cake near the size of Boston. He saw it was me and his smile faded.

Clearing my throat, I said, "Brother Clyde, Mama told me about the Sandwich Islands and you and her. I've been thinking, and I know . . . I mean, I love my pa and . . . I mean . . ." I cleared my throat again; by that time the entire table was silent, waiting to hear what in thunder I *did* mean. "In a way you're already part of this family. If I can't have my real pa, I guess I'd rather you than anyone. But I can't call you Pa."

Mama started to say something, but Brother Clyde gently touched her arm. "Thank you entirely for the welcome, missy. I'm mighty pleased to be part of this family. And I don't expect you to call me Pa. Why don't you just call me Brother? Growing up I had seven sisters and they all called me Brother. It seemed natural to be Brother Clyde when I took up the Lord's work, and I'd be right proud to be Brother to you, too."

"I can't say I think much of this Sandwich Island plan," I added, "but if Mama wants to go, I guess we go." Then I leaned down, kissed his cheek, and ran for my bed, where I alternately cried and slept until morning, feeling every so often Mama or Brother Clyde or both of them together smooth my covers and touch my hair. "You were right, Pa," I whispered to the redbearded man whose face I could not see.

CHAPTER EIGHTEEN

SUMMER 1852
In which I say good-bye

Brother Claymore prepared to make his rounds about the mountains and the rivers again, this time to raise the money to take us to the Sandwich Islands. "Full as I am of the spirit of God, I feel I could swim there and live on locusts and wild honey like the prophets of old, but I can't ask that of my family," he told Jimmy, as they tied Clyde's belongings onto tiny Apostle. "I know my brother miners will want to help send forth to the glory of God me and these innocent children and my wife-to-be, the lovely Mrs. Whipple."

"Sister Whipple," Mama said. Then, her eyes bright and merry, "Sister Claymore." After Brother Clyde left, Mama spent an unseemly amount of time looking off into the distance and sighing.

I would have liked to write to Gram and tell her about the fire, Mama marrying Clyde, and my banishment to the Sandwich Islands, where I would face a future going barefoot and eating coconuts like Robinson Crusoe. But I couldn't. I had no paper, no ink, and no Snowshoe to carry a letter to San Francisco. So instead I climbed up the ravine as far as I could on the path soggy with ash and mud, and called to her: "Gra-a-a-am, it's me, Lu-u-cy. I ne-e-e-ed you." I knew she couldn't hear me, but I felt better anyway. I added, just in case, "Please send some a-a-a-pples and chicken ste-w-w!"

July came to Lucky Diggins while Mama waited for Brother Clyde to return and I just waited. Meanwhile, a miracle was bringing books back to me, books that had survived the fire because they had not been in the boarding house but in some miner's tent far up the river, books that arrived from Sacramento or San Francisco, sent by someone who had borrowed one in the past and wanted to replace what was lost, books handed from miner to miner over the unpassable mountains. I sniffed them, read a little, packed them in a potato sack, and waited some more.

"If we're going to go, I wish to goodness we'd just go," I told Lizzie one day while we sewed a patch on the ceiling of the tent.

"You don't sound too happy about going."

"Doesn't seem to matter."

"I guess you're not much for adventures. Are you afraid?"

"Yes, I'm afraid. I'm afraid I'll never get home to Massachusetts now. The Sandwich Islands must be half a world away."

"So don't go," Lizzie said.

"And I sure don't look forward to another boat trip and starting all over again to make friends and settle in."

"You know, you don't *have* to go."

"Well, of course I do. I have to go. Don't I?" I said to Lizzie. Don't I? I said to myself.

Lizzie looked at me in a way that made me desperate to change the subject.

"Who is more handsome, Rusty or Snoose McGrath?" I asked her.

"The Gent," answered Lizzie.

"Well, of course you'd say that. You're sweet on him."

"Rubbish," said Lizzie. "How about you, Miss Lucy? Who do you think is handsome?"

"Nobody here. All boneheads and bandits." I thought sometimes about falling in love, but only late at night in the dark where no one could see me blush. I could imagine Ivanhoe and Rowena kissing and making sweet noises to each other, but Lucy Whipple and some miner? Not likely. "Anyway, I'm off to the Sandwich Islands, where I'll probably marry a coconut farmer and eat dried fish and never have a new book to read." I pushed the needle so fiercely through the dingy canvas that I near sewed my finger to the tent and faced having to stay in Lucky Diggins until one of us rotted away.

"Those books sure mean a lot to you," Lizzie said later as she left. "I can think of lots of things I'd miss more than books if I was dragged across the ocean to some island."

"Who's going to what island?" It was Belle Scatter-that-was, cradling a puny, red, squalling infant in her arms. Little fond as I was of Belle, hers was the first new face I had seen since the fire. I made Belle sit down and tell me about her married life and what in tarnation she was doing back in this Godforsaken ash heap and had she brought chicken or cheese or paper and pens, while I took and comforted the baby. Belle obviously still needed more practice.

"There's some boxes over to my Pa's tent," said Belle. "Me and Mr. Rush and Fanny Melinda came to visit and say good-bye. Too many lawyers coming to California. Besides, I think it's no fit place to rear a child, so we're going east, to New York." Belle's face was as shiny bright as a new skillet. "Imagine, New York. Indoor privies and horse-drawn carriages and big hats with flowers."

Back east. While I was heading into *Robinson Crusoe* country, Belle was going to New York to wear a big flowered hat in her indoor privy!

She moved to take Fanny Melinda back, and the

baby started up her squalling and fussing again. "Seems to me," I said, bouncing the little mite, "this little one is a mighty big handful. How are you going to manage her all the way across the country to New York?"

"Well," Belle said, with a cunning look on her face, "that's why I come over here to see you. I know you been hankerin' to go back to Massachusetts since you got here. What about you leaving with us? If your mama says yes, we would chaperone and pay your way in exchange for your being nursemaid to Fanny Melinda." She smiled at the baby in my arms, and the baby started to scream again.

"Belle! Truly?" I danced Fanny Melinda around that tent as if we were at the Governor's Ball. "When? Oh, when would we go?"

"After trekking in on that measly, burned-out path, I don't hanker to trek on out again. We'll wait until wagons can get through; should be soon now. Week or two or three."

Didn't sound so soon to me, but it was the best offer I had got in a long time. We shook hands on the deal and I danced all the way home. I was going back to Massachusetts!

"Hallelujah and good-bye, California!" I called. "Good riddance to ash and dust and mud. Good-bye, yellow hills and dry, cracked earth, pinecones and acorn cakes, evergreens, mountain peaks, and blue blue sky! Good-bye, Goldometers and Rattlesnake Jake," I added, laughing, "and the dag diggety miner in his union suit. Good-bye long soft autumn nights and the smell of pines and the hills ablaze with poppies." My dancing got slower and quieter. "Good-bye, Jimmy and Lizzie and the Gent . . ." I sighed and went the rest of the way in silence.

When I got home, there was Brother Claymore back, sitting on the floor of the tent, head in his hands. Mama was saying, "It don't matter, Clyde. We don't need to go anywhere; we can get married and open the boarding house again." He looked stricken, so Mama took a breath and said, "Or we can wait until you raise the rest of the money. I know there aren't many people around, and those that are can't give like they used to, but we're not old. We can wait a year or two." And at that they both looked stricken.

"Mama," I said, "you don't need as much passage money as you thought. I'm not going with you. I have made arrangements to go back east with Belle Scatter. I'm finally going home, Mama!"

It was quiet as spring rain. You couldn't even hear breathing. I finally said, "Mama?"

"Clyde will get the rest of the money. He can sell Apostle. When he comes back, we must all be ready. Now Lucy, have you—"

"Mama? Didn't you hear me?"

"I heard wind strring the trees, squirrels chattering over nuts, the river rippling through the rocks. I did not hear a foolish thing like you saying you're not going with us."

"What about my standing like a tub on my own bottom?"

"You can stand like a tub just fine in the Sandwich Islands, thank you very much. Now no more talking about it."

"But Mama . . ."

"But Mama nothing. I swear when I die that will be carved on my tombstone. 'But Mama.'"

"Mama, sit down. I want to say something."

"Lucy, I don't have time for your wobblies."

"Mama, sit!" And which of us was more surprised when Mama obeyed I couldn't tell. "Going west again is Brother Clyde's dream, and yours, not mine. I am going home."

Mama opened her mouth to speak again but nothing came out.

"Never thought I'd see you speechless, Mama."

"Never thought I'd see you turning your back on your own family. . . ."

"Now, Mama, it will be all right. Prairie is big enough to help you, and Sierra is nearly six, and you will have Brother Clyde, too. I'll give you the money left from my pickle crock. I won't need it. Go west and find your heart's desire. And let me find mine."

"But California . . ."

"But California nothing, Mama."

After a supper of rabbit and acorn mash and cheese from Belle, we all sat around the tree-stump table while Mama counted out the nuggets and coins in the pickle crock and added it to what Brother Clyde had collected. We figured the dust at a dollar a pinch and added it in. Not enough. Mama sighed and counted again. Still not enough. Brother Clyde put his arm around Mama, Prairie cried a little, and Sierra did too, because Prairie did.

Jimmy Whiskers took Mama's hand and said, "Listen, Arvella, I think you counted wrong. Let me have a try." So he picked up the dust and coins and tiny nuggets in his dirty brown palm and counted again. And, like the miracle of loaves and fishes in the Bible, lo, there was enough!

"Now how did I miss counting those big nuggets there?" Mama asked as Prairie and Sierra jumped up and down, shrieking in glee.

Jimmy just shrugged and smiled. His front teeth were gone. He winked at me.

A few days and Mama and Clyde, Prairie and Sierra, would be gone, heading for San Francisco, where Brother and Mama could be married by a preacher before they all boarded a ship carrying hides, calico, lumber, and missionaries to the Sandwich Islands. Although wagons couldn't get through yet, the paths were clear enough for folks and mules, so they made plans for crossing the mountains to Marysville with others who were leaving: Poker John Lewis and Milly from the saloon, who were going to San Francisco to marry and open a card parlor; Ripley Gurgins, who had his eye on a German widow and her farm over near Colusa; Billy and Beppie Parker, going home to Indiana, and Amos Frogge on to Colorado. Even Flapjack, who said he had been in the mountains longer than God, left, saying with a smack of his empty gums, "I'm going to find me some gold easier to dig." It looked like Lucky Diggins was plumb closing down.

The morning of their departure I walked with Mama, Clyde, Prairie, and Sierra to where the group waited at the foot of the ravine path. The girls were lifted onto Apostle's back, and Mama carried what little she owned in a sack made from a tent that had been made from a blanket that had once most likely been something else. How could they venture over the burned-out, pathless mountains and the unknown sea like this, so vulnerable and so poor? I kissed Clyde on the cheek and said, "Take good care of them."

Clyde tipped his hat and said, "God and I will both watch over them, Sister Lucy. With the help of Bernard Whipple from Heaven."

"Prairie," I said, hugging her, "help Mama like I did."

Prairie's eyes twinkled behind her spectacles.

"You're right," I admitted. "That wouldn't be hard. Help Mama better than I did." I hugged her sturdy little body.

"And you, Sierra . . ."

"We're going on a boat, Luthy." It was Sierra's turn to lose a tooth. I felt so old. "We're going to thee whaleth and gullth and pick bread from treeth."

Jimmy Whiskers kissed Sierra and Prairie and even Mama, saying, "Sorry you have to go, Arvella, just when your bread was gettin' fit to eat."

Mama hugged me and we both started crying. Then she stood back and looked at me. Really looked at me. "I've never known quite what to make of you, girl. I was so afraid you were weak and dreamy like your pa."

"Mama! Pa wasn't weak—"

"Lucy, allow me to know something. You're not the only smart one here."

"But Mama," I said, as much for old times' sake as for the argument, and we both laughed while we cried.

"You're just like your pa in some ways, my girl. Many of them good." Mama hugged me again. "But mostly you're like me. Isn't that a corker?"

I grabbed Mama then and held on like I was drowning. "Mama, when will I see you again?"

Tears ran down Mama's face. "We're going to the Sandwich Islands, Lucy, not dying. We'll see you again. We got to. We're family."

Mama turned to head up the path, then turned back to me and opened her mouth. I stopped her, straightened her sack, and said, "Go, Mama. I'll cry sometimes and miss you like anything, but don't worry. I'll be fine." That was mostly to reassure Mama, but as I said it, I realized it was true. I'd be fine. Soon as the way was clear, Belle and Mr. Rush and Fanny Melinda and I would be getting in a wagon, heading east, going home.

When the group had struggled up the ravine path and disappeared into the trees, it was all I could do to keep from running after them. Mama, gone! And Prairie and Sierra! And Bernard, Snowshoe, and Amos Frogge! I felt so alone, I went out to the meadow and had a long talk with Butte and a good cry.

CHAPTER NINETEEN

SUMMER-AUTUMN 1852
In which I am home at last

It was so quiet with Mama, Clyde, and the girls gone. I decided to move in with Belle and her family so Jimmy and the Gent could have our tent. Other than trying to keep Fanny Melinda dry and quiet, I had nothing much to do, no miners to feed or quilts to patch or sisters to mind, so I wandered often through the hills yellow in the summer sun, looking and thinking.

Then, the last week of July, Belle said that her pa had asked Mrs. Flagg to marry him and she, still silent, had nodded, and the wedding was to be on August 1. Mr. Scatter, as self-proclaimed mayor of Lucky Diggins, named Jimmy a justice of the peace so he could do the honors.

August 1 dawned so hot and dry the ground cracked, and there were more ants and lizards at the ceremony by the river than guests, but a good time was had by all. Or almost all. I kept thinking about Mama and Clyde and the wedding I was missing: Ma in a new flowered hat, her hand in Brother Clyde's big paw; a smiling Prairie and Sierra standing by Apostle, who'd be decorated for the occasion with flowers and maybe bells in his bridle. I had to think hard about Gram and Rocky Flat and the lending library to keep my eyes dry.

The fire having taken everything, the Flagg-and-Scatter wedding was not the world's fanciest. Mrs. Flagg wore the old blue dress that used to be mine. With a pink ribbon of Belle's around her waist and wild roses in her hair, she looked pretty and summery and happy. Lizzie and Ruby Ramona were clean and tidy and relieved about not being "all ragged out in fancy doodads." They stood hand in hand behind their mother, trying to look ordinary and unexcited, but the big smiles on their faces when she whispered "I do" lit up the foothills all the way to Marysville.

Afterward folk hollered, "Speech! Speech!" and Rusty fired his pistol into the air.

"Shut up, you coyotes, and give a man a chance to talk," said Mr. Scatter. "I have something important to say." He looked at Mrs. Flagg—Mrs. Scatter, that is—and they smiled at each other. "We been talking. Seems like after all we've been through here, this place is home—in adverse circumstances right now, but home. And we don't aim to see it go down without a fight." He picked up a piece of charcoal and wrote on the lone wall of the saloon, OPEN FOR BIZNESS. "We got little to offer but hope, a few boxes and barrels, and a case of Professor Terence O'Hare's World-Famous Pile and Humor Cure," said Mr. Scatter with a grin, "but we ain't leaving Lucky Diggins. Why, I ain't even rich yet."

Folks cheered again, although I myself could not see cheering about staying put in Lucky Diggins. Jimmy lit the torches along the riverbank, the Gent played his homemade fiddle like a devil was in him, and there was dancing and tomfoolery.

I kind of hung around the edges, missing Mama and feeling too lonely to celebrate, but Jimmy Whiskers insisted, so I twirled with Jimmy and Snoose McGrath and even the new bridegroom, Mr. Scatter, who said he was "so peedoodled before the ceremony I near put my pants on upside down."

Finally the Gent gave his fiddle to Rusty and commenced dancing with Lizzie, and it seemed like they would never stop. Sure enough, next morning Lizzie told me that she and the Gent were getting married in the fall, and they were going to farm in Live Oak Valley, right across the river. "The Gent can't mine no more with his bad feet and rheumatics and all, but we ain't givin' up on this town neither. My brothers are going to stay and help us, and someday our kids." She had a gooney sort of look on her face that reminded me of Mama looking at Clyde. A rush of loneliness nearly overwhelmed me.

"When's this wagon going to be arriving?" I asked Belle next day, mighty sick of sitting around and bouncing Fanny Melinda. "Been longer than a week or two, hasn't it?"

"Guess it'll get here when it gets here," she said, which was no help at all. "I just hope it comes before the rains do, or we'll be stuck until next year. No mule will be able to cross the mountains on those wet, gummy paths, much less a wagon."

Next year! I wished then I was more of a one for praying, but I feared God hardly even knew my name by now.

One morning Mr. Scatter stopped to talk to me. He wanted a sign for the new general store ("Lucky Diggins General Store, Mr. and Mrs. Leon Scatter, Props."), and he wanted me to write it so all the words would be spelled right.

It seemed to me the rebuilding of the general store after the conflagration we had endured called for more than just "Mr. and Mrs. Leon Scatter, Props." Perhaps a heroic poem, something like "Old Ironsides" or "Excelsior."

I labored long and hard, writing and rewriting, crossing out and scratching in. When it was finished, Snoose McGrath helped me paint it on a board with paint made from red clay and tree sap. After most of three days, it was finished. I wrapped the sign in a potato sack and carried it to Mr. Scatter.

"Whatcha got there, little sister?" Jimmy called as I passed him.

"A sign for Mr. Scatter's store."

"Whoo-ha! This I gotta see!" Jimmy fell in behind me.

"Where you goin', Jimmy?" asked Rusty, carrying water back from the river.

"Unveiling a great work of art," Jimmy answered. Rusty joined us, as did a group of miners standing jawing in the shade. We looked like an Independence Day Parade, only poky and more shabby.

Mr. Scatter was so excited over his sign, he ripped the sack right off and read it out loud, stopping for words he didn't know and whispering those he wasn't sure of. He looked at me, snuffled, and read it again, in a loud ringing voice:

> "Beans and Bacon, Fish in Cans,
> Barrels of Flour, Sacks of Yams,
> Raisins, Rice, Salt Pork, and Such,
> Wools and Cottons, Soft to Touch.
> Tubs and Buckets, Pots and Pans,
> Gulls' Eggs from the Farallons.
> Kegs of Whiskey, Candy Treats,
> Picks and Shovels, Pickled Beets.
> We take Credit, Coins, and Dust.
> Come to Scatter's, a Store to Trust."

Well, you would have thought old Henry W. Longfellow himself had come to declaim *Evangeline*, there was such cheering and laughing and carrying on. It didn't even seem to matter that some of the rhymes were wrong, that Mr. Scatter's store didn't have any of the things advertised, or that I promised credit from a man who wouldn't give credit to the archangel Gabriel. I figured it was time he did.

Mr. Scatter had to read it over and over, and I had to read it twice. Everyone but the Esteemed Author then retired to the shade of a burned-out oak to break into one of the scorched but intact bottles of whiskey found, like buried treasure, in the ashes of the saloon.

Then, on a Monday morning, while Fanny Melinda blew spit bubbles and pulled my hair, the future rode into town. The wagon trail from Marysville had finally been cleared, and here came a train of mules laden with food and other goods, wagons creaking under their loads of tools and machinery, and, at the head, like a Roman emperor leading a triumphal procession, a small bald man in a stiff black suit, sitting on a mule, puffing on a cigar, and singing "Away up on the Yuba River."

"Agamemnon Porterhouse," he said to Mr. Scatter, "at your service. I represent the Green Mountain Investment Company of Poxley, Vermont, and we have come to scout a promising location for the largest hard-rock mine north of Bailey Pines." Jimmy and the Gent stopped working, Mr. Scatter left off arguing with

Snoose McGrath, Fanny Melinda let go of my hair, everyone in town, in fact, dropped what they were doing and came over to hear Agamemnon Porterhouse talk.

"Seems you hereabouts got the land and the mountains and the quartz rock heavy with gold," he said, "but no way to get to it. We propose to buy up your land, stake whatever further claims we still can, tunnel deep into the mountains, and use that there machinery to bring out the rock by the ton and crush it to extract the gold. You profit, gentlemen, Lucky Diggins profits, and, of course, the Green Mountain Investment Company profits." He took a puff of his cigar and blew a perfect smoke ring into the clear sweet air.

Waiting at the top of the ravine path—as close to Lucky Diggins as it could get—was a stagecoach, the first seen in these mountains. Jimmy and I climbed up to take a closer look. The coach was canary yellow with four enormous iron-bound wooden wheels. Even dirty and scraped and scarred, with broken seats and a team of tired horses, it was a blame sight more elegant than a mule and rickety buckboard.

The stage driver brought news: Flapjack had been shot in San Francisco by a lady gambler, Bean Belly Thompson had been bit so hard by one of his mules that he couldn't sit down and was going out of the hauling business, and our runaway boarder Percival Coogan had died in Sacramento of throat trouble.

"Quinsy?" Mr. Scatter asked.

"Hangin'," the stage driver replied.

"Told you," I whispered to Butte in my mind.

The stage also brought Mrs. Porterhouse, three small boys, and so much baggage it looked like they meant to stay a good long while. Took all day for Jimmy, Rusty, and Snoose to pack that stuff—and Mrs. Porterhouse, a stout and stately lady—down the ravine path.

Now that the way was open, some miners went home with their profits. Others, unwilling to work for someone else, went to Gravel Bar or Bedbug Flat or somewhere unknown and unnamed but rich with the promise of easy gold. The rest sold their claims to the mining company and learned to fix and run and clean the machines that dammed the river and crushed the rock. And that's how the Green Mountain Investment Company of Poxley, Vermont, ended up owning so much of the California land that the Americans had taken from the Mexicans who had taken it from the Spanish who had taken it from the Indians and the salmon and the bears.

But all that was yet to come. Right now the stage was leaving for Skunk Valley and assorted other stops. When it returned in two days, I would get on it with Belle and her family. We'd take the stage to Sacramento, then hire a wagon and team for the trip to St. Louis, where we'd board the train for New York; in only eight weeks or so, I'd be home. My heart thumped with excitement, but I was a little bit sorry to leave so soon.

Changes were coming to Lucky Diggins, and I was mighty curious to see what would happen.

Next afternoon a strange miner appeared at the tent with a wrapped package. "You the gal they call little sister?" he asked me.

"Unfortunately so," I answered.

"That mean yes or no?"

"Yes. They call me little sister."

"Well, I ran into a fella in New Orleans, me coming to California and him going home. He gave me this here parcel and asked would I deliver it to little sister of Lucky Diggins, near Marysville, in California. So I done it and now I'm off." He tipped his head and walked away before I could say "Howdy" or "Thank you" or "Have an onion or some beans."

I ripped the parcel open. It was a copy of *Ivanhoe*. Inside was a note:

Little sister,

I heared you was burned out. I'm sorry for the loss of yer books. You never met me but I read this book of yers once in California. Borryed it from someone who borryed it from someone who knew someone who knew you. When I saw a schoolteacher fella in Missouri with the same book, I thought it should go to little sister, to replace the one the fire et up. So here it is back again. Didn't take too much to persuade the schoolteacher to part with it. He was a puny fella.

Yer friend, Maxwell Parsons

I sat for a long time reading *Ivanhoe* and then, strangely restless, went for my last walk in Lucky Diggins. I climbed up the ravine path to the top and looked around. Hawks danced in the relentless, endless, cloudless blue sky. In the distance the hills were turning yellow with wild oats and ripening grasses. Here and there patches of growing things had escaped the fire: late-blooming gentians, asters, goldenrods, mosses, and liverworts. Lizards scampered over the dry, cracked ground.

Around a bend I came upon a fawn. She looked closely at me and then, startled by my human smell, tried to run, tripped over a branch, and fell to the ground flat, four legs splayed out around her. Before I could move, she was up again and took off into the brush. Why was she alone? Had she lost her mama? Or was she on her own, maybe for the first time?

The sun set rose and crimson over the dark mountains that stood watching over me. "Magnificent," I said to a lizard who was sunning on my boot. "And beautiful. But you better move now. It's getting late and I have to go on home." And I did, surprised at my choice of words.

I climbed down to Lucky Diggins, the gold and dusty air fragrant with the smell of pines, mint, and ripening berries. From the shacks and tents came laughter and the clanking of tin dishes as folks got ready for supper. Rusty's mouth harp sang, accompanied by the honking of wild geese. I could smell burned beans and mules and privies. It all seemed as familiar as morning, and I was filled with happiness, sadness, and something powerful but nameless.

Dear Mama,

I picture you standing barefoot on a beach with wind blowing your hair and a coconut in your hand. I reckon you have never been so happy. Except for missing you something fierce, I am happy, too.

I have things to tell you. I hope there are places to sit there in the Sandwich Islands, for I suggest you sit now.

I joined Belle and her husband and Fanny Melinda at Mr. Scatter's, ready to climb up to where the stagecoach waited. Jimmy and the Gent had come to see me off, the Gent with an armload of wild sunflowers and Jimmy awash in tears. Lizzie and her ma, who is now Mrs. Scatter, watched quietly from inside the store. No one was smiling or patting me on the back. It felt like a funeral.

And then, Mama, all the thinking I had been doing while I waited suddenly came together, like the pots and pans melted in the fire. And there it was. I realized that east isn't home, Massachusetts isn't home. Home is you and Pa, Butte, Prairie, Sierra, and the baby Golden, Gram and Grampop. The Massachusetts that is home is in my heart, not a town forty miles west of Boston. And I can take it with me wherever I go, but I can never go back there again.

Seems to me home is where I am loved and safe and needed. And that's Lucky Diggins. Finally, Mama, Lucky Diggins is home and I'm not going anywhere after all.

I tried to explain this to Belle. I'm not sure she understood, but she wished me luck and began to bounce Fanny Melinda. Marriage sure has softened her edges.

I was mighty regretful for a while after they left, being all alone here with no Mama, no pickle crock, and no hope for Massachusetts. I thought I had made a prodigious mistake. What was I to do? I didn't hanker to spend my days baking pies.

I talked to Lizzie and to Butte and read the Ivanhoe *sent me from New Orleans and then was inspired. I went to see this Mrs. Porterhouse, who came to town with the Green Mountain Investment Company to save Lucky Diggins. She said their entire Vermont house is being shipped in pieces around the Horn and up the trail to Lucky Diggins for rebuilding. Can you imagine? What a sight. She's determined to civilize California, starting with Lucky Diggins, and is campaigning for a school and a real brick church. So I told her my inspiration: a lending library in the church basement. She said, "Lucille," her being a grand and formal kind of person, "Lucille, girl, you think like me." You could tell she meant it as a compliment. I hugged her so tight I almost burst her corset.*

I have spoken to the miners left around here and some farmers in the valley. They agree to pay a dollar a month apiece to run the library and pay a librarian. We do not have many books yet, just mine that have come back and some books on manners and household decoration that Mrs. Porterhouse brought. But we will. For one, I am donating Ivanhoe.

I am Miss Whipple, town librarian! Lizzie is helping me sew a shirtwaist with a high collar and long skirts, suitable for a professional. I will stay right here in a room over the general store and run the library, ordering books and mending torn pages, keeping track of who borrows what, reading whatever I like, living and working surrounded by books. Mama, imagine. It is my heart's desire. My real heart's desire.

Last Sunday I was missing you all so much, I went again to be with Butte. Mr. Scatter is building a great house right over the spot where the boarding house was, so I dug up the flower bulbs and planted them on Butte's grave. He will have flowers come spring. And I brought him a present: antifogmatic, the fifty-first word for liquor. From Mr. Porterhouse. Butte must be plumb tickled.

Give my love to Brother Clyde and Prairie and Sierra. I think of you all the time and cry sometimes, and I worry about you there in the wilderness without me. But I am doing fine on my own.

> *Yours truly,*
> *Your loving daughter,*
> *Miss California Morning Whipple,*
> *happy citizen and librarian of*
> *Lucky Diggins, California, U.S.A.*

187

Author's Note

The story of the California gold rush has always been as much myth as history. The myth says that the Gold Rush consisted entirely of men who left home and family to strike it rich in California. Indeed, I discovered an 1850 census that estimated that ninety percent of those who came to California to search for gold were male. But what about the other ten percent? They were wives, mothers, sisters, daughters, and sometimes women like Arvella Whipple who came without a man. They walked across the country in long skirts and long hair, bore babies on the trail or in brush huts along rivers, cooked and washed for their own families and as many other prospectors as they could to earn money. I admired the strength and courage of these women and of the children who crossed the continent with baby sisters and brothers on their shoulders or in their arms. Theirs was the story that interested me and led me in search of Lucy Whipple and her mother.

California itself has long been a land of myth, from as far back as its naming in the seventeenth century for the fictional Queen Calafia, ruler of a mysterious island inhabited by tall bronze Amazons. Spanish explorers, following a map that depicted California as an island in the Pacific, came looking for the legendary Seven Cities of Cibola, the kingdom of La Gran Quivara, and the fabled El Dorado, places of untold wealth where even the kitchen utensils were made of gold.

The myth also tells us that the Spanish "discovered" the land known as California. Obviously it had already been found by the native peoples who had been there for hundreds—perhaps thousands—of years. The Spanish met, defeated, and enslaved them, and then Mexico revolted against Spain and took California for its own.

Despite the myth that Americans "settled" California, and in violation of their own treaty, the United States actually conquered and annexed it from the Mexicans who had taken it from the Spanish. Those who suffered the greatest losses in this shifting and reshifting were the California Indians, who numbered over 360,000 in the early 1800s but fewer than 15,000 by 1900. The Maidu, the native people who lived in the area of the gold rush, numbered 9,000 before the white men came. By 1856 6,000 Maidu were dead or gone. The native Californians lost their land, had no legal rights in the new state of California, and were beaten, enslaved, or killed by violence or disease.

The lumps of gold lying in the streams and fields of the California mountains were also mythical. The fantasy of easy gold was a "carnival of hope" that lured more than 300,000 people to California by 1853.

Most of those who came were searching for gold, not putting down roots or building homes. When they realized that gold was hard dug and hard won, not lying around for the picking up, most left. Ninety percent of the population of Grass Valley, a typical mining town, in 1850 was gone by 1856. Those who stayed became Californians. They opened stores and lumberyards, brickyards and iron foundries. They ran newspapers and banks or turned to teaching and farming.

The myth also claimed that mining put all men on the same level. Supposedly, family, background, manners, and looks didn't count for much: Anyone could strike it rich. In truth this did not extend to those not white or not American. The gold rush story is filled with tales of riots, fights, and murder, not only over gold but over race and color. The Fugitive Slave Laws worked against blacks seeking freedom, and the repressive Foreign Miners' Tax was enforced primarily upon the Chinese and Hispanics.

The real gold in California proved to be the rich, fertile land. The farms, cattle ranches, and orange groves of the new Californians grew into today's multibillion-dollar agribusiness.

The gold rush, which brought thousands to live on

and off the land, also brought ecological disaster. Miners stripped the soil, leaving behind piles of refuse and rusting machinery. Creek beds were mangled by massive dredges. Giant hoses pounded the hillsides with millions of gallons of water, turning rivers into mud. Mountains were torn down and the courses of rivers changed. Years of mindless waste and pollution damaged and destroyed wildlife and natural resources. Parts of California were ravaged, used up, and left to die.

The gold rush's promise of easy money—whether myth or not—affected people's values and expectations. It was another manifestation of the nineteenth-century belief that anyone could get rich in America. Gone was the Old Country and its fixed economic and social classes. Americans believed they were free to choose their lives, better their conditions.

Politicians and preachers claimed that the New World offered an abundance of riches for the taking, and the optimistic, opportunistic Americans took them. Those who went to the gold fields believed they had a right to the land and its wealth, no matter whose it had been before.

Perhaps even more than the gold, it was the promise of opportunity that brought so many to California. In 1850 California was so populous and powerful and so desirable to the United States that it became the thirty-first state in the Union, the only state in the west not to have been a territory first.

The different kinds of people who came to California brought a diversity of cultures—and culture. California was not merely made up of those frontiersmen who pushed on from other areas of the west. California attracted easterners, midwesterners, southerners, Europeans, Asians, South and Central Americans—a mix of people from all over the world who brought their own cultural influences. Newspapers, literature, theater, and opera flourished, a situation you wouldn't think to find on the "frontier."

One of the fruits of this transplanting of culture was the library. New England had had subscription libraries in meeting halls and coffee houses for a century. In 1834 Peterborough, New Hampshire, began the nation's first free public library. Those westerners who like Lucy had grown up with the libraries of the east were anxious to bring them to California. Libraries sprang up in some gold rush towns as early as 1849.

Lucy Whipple personifies the gold rush pioneers. She came to California to get rich and get out; yet beguiled by the land and the people, she stayed to be a Californian and enrich her new home with the experiences, culture, and expectations she brought with her.

I tried in this book to use language, ideas, and attitudes contemporary to 1850s California. For example, African-Americans are referred to as colored instead of black or Negro, which were considered derogatory terms at the time. Slang, swear words, and odd turns of phrase were found in or inspired by the reference works *Wicked Words: A Treasury of Curses, Insults, Put-Downs, and Other Formerly Unprintable Terms* by Hugh Rawson (Crown Publishers, 1989); *Cowboy Slang* by Edgar R. "Frosty" Potter (Golden West Publishers, 1986); and *The Writer's Guide to Everyday Life in the 1800s* by Marc McCutcheon (Writers' Digest Books, 1993).

There are many, many books on the California gold rush, but very few of them discuss the children of the time. Some of the most helpful California books I found included:

Chauncey Canfield: *The Diary of a Forty-Niner.* Turtle Point Press, 1992.

"Dame Shirley": *The Shirley Letters from the California Mines.* Knopf, 1965.

Joy Hakim: *A History of Us, Book Five: Liberty for All?* Oxford University Press, 1994.

Robert F. Heizer and Albert B. Elsasser: *The Natural World of the California Indians.* University of California Press, 1980.

Joseph Henry Jackson: *Anybody's Gold: The History of California's Mining Towns.* Chronicle, 1970.

Joann Levy: *They Saw the Elephant: Women in the Califonia Gold Rush.* Archon, 1990.

Remi Nadeau: *Ghost Towns and Mining Camps of California.* Crest, 1992.

Petra Press: *A Multicultural Portrait of the Move West*. Marshall Cavendish, 1994.

Sarah Royce: *A Frontier Lady*. University of Nebraska Press, 1932.

Lillian Schlissel: *Women's Diaries of the Westward Journey*. Schocken, 1992.

Elliott West: *Growing Up with the Country: Childhood on the Far Western Frontier*. University of New Mexico Press, 1989.

U.S. President James K. Polk claimed the California gold discoveries were "the find of the century." An early miner said gold meant "castles of marble . . . thousands of slaves . . . myriads of fair virgins contending with each other for my love." The Sioux holy man Black Elk called gold the yellow metal that makes the white man crazy. I think perhaps they were all correct.